A Wild Scotswoman

She drew a furious breath. "*I* restrain myself? *I*? I am not foolish, and neither are you! How *dare* you touch your *future stepmother*?"

"Perhaps," he said quietly, "it is because she is no more a lady than I am a gentleman." He stood silently, hands at his sides, watching her in the dark.

Hugging herself in the cool night air, she clenched her fists, hating the swell of tears behind her eyelids. *The devil take him. I will not cry. I shall prove him wrong—and make him take back every word.*

He waited and, when she did not respond, bent down, picked up his coat from the grass, and lightly slipped it around her shoulders once more.

"I am trying to save you a great deal of difficulty," he said soberly. "You shall not last here above a fortnight. Your chances of becoming my stepmother are no better than those of becoming my wife."

Cora inhaled sharply. The wild Scotswoman within her rose with sword brandished.

"*Your* wife? When horses *fly*, sirrah!"

When Horses Fly

Laurie Bishop

A SIGNET BOOK

SIGNET
Published by New American Library, a division of
Penguin Group (USA) Inc., 375 Hudson Street,
New York, New York 10014, USA
Penguin Group (Canada), 90 Eglinton Avenue East, Suite 700, Toronto,
Ontario M4P 2Y3, Canada (a division of Pearson Penguin Canada Inc.)
Penguin Books Ltd., 80 Strand, London WC2R 0RL, England
Penguin Ireland, 25 St. Stephen's Green, Dublin 2,
Ireland (a division of Penguin Books Ltd.)
Penguin Group (Australia), 250 Camberwell Road, Camberwell, Victoria 3124,
Australia (a division of Pearson Australia Group Pty. Ltd.)
Penguin Books India Pvt. Ltd., 11 Community Centre, Panchsheel Park,
New Delhi - 110 017, India
Penguin Group (NZ), cnr Airborne and Rosedale Roads, Albany,
Auckland 1310, New Zealand (a division of Pearson New Zealand Ltd.)
Penguin Books (South Africa) (Pty.) Ltd., 24 Sturdee Avenue,
Rosebank, Johannesburg 2196, South Africa

Penguin Books Ltd., Registered Offices:
80 Strand, London WC2R 0RL, England

First published by Signet, an imprint of New American Library,
a division of Penguin Group (USA) Inc.

First Printing, October 2005
10 9 8 7 6 5 4 3 2 1

Ⓟ REGISTERED TRADEMARK—MARCA REGISTRADA

Printed in the United States of America

*In Memory of Frederick J. Bishop,
husband, scholar, and friend.
He taught me how to laugh
and to cherish today.*

Chapter One

For a young woman who had lived the whole of her life in the Yorkshire dales, the long coach trip south would have been daunting in the best of circumstances. But Cora MacLaren was alone, and the fact that she would no longer be alone upon her arrival in Beachy Head was of no real reassurance. She was going to live with an elderly distant cousin whom she had never seen—and he was, from all she had heard, an eccentric recluse.

She had it from her late great-aunt and patient, Mrs. Leyburn, that Lord Wintercroft was a cross old miser who lived in a stone pile of an old castle in Sussex, had been widowed many years, and had never remarried. This, however, had not dissuaded Great-aunt Leyburn from writing Lord Wintercroft when it seemed that shortly Cora would be requiring a new position.

Great-aunt Leyburn, her frail old body propped up by pillows in her bed, had dictated while Cora wrote, and Cora had uttered not one word of objection. Cora had already stayed with several relatives who were known to her, practicing her levelheaded resourcefulness and her medical arts until they no longer had need of her. She did not know anyone she might go to after Aunt Leyburn; and after all, as Aunt pointed out, Lord Wintercroft was head of the family.

Still, it was a surprise when Lord Wintercroft replied with the offer of a home for Cora—rather than the offer of a position. It seemed particularly odd from a man reputed to be so tightfisted, enough so that refusal crossed her mind; but with her poor Great-aunt Leyburn on her deathbed expressing such satisfaction at the outcome of her last act in this life, Cora consented. Besides, Cora reasoned that Lord Wintercroft was in probable need of good nursing care, and his object was likely to avoid engaging her services for pay, although she had never expected any. Cora was a country doctor's daughter, and she was an excellent nurse.

Therefore, as the coach rumbled to a stop at the tiny hamlet of Croft's Corners, Cora had no illusions about what she could expect at the old man's home. *I might be swallowed up by the pile of ancient rock and never see the light of day again.*

Pricked by the humor of the thought, Cora smiled, picturing her unromantic self as the heroine of *The Castle of Otranto*, which she had read aloud to her Great-aunt Leyburn. She was hardly Walpole's Isabella. On the other hand, her new home might prove an interesting sort of challenge. Her father, God rest his soul, had taught her to appreciate challenges; he had taught her courage as well.

"Step lively! Step lively!" The old woman with whom she had shared her inside bench jabbed her in the arm. "They dunna' hold here. You make haste an' get down."

Cora grabbed her satchel and her precious bundle of books. Standing at a half crouch, struggling past the woman's knees and those of the farmer opposite, she made it to the coach door just as the guard was picking up the step.

"Oh, wait!" She gestured desperately, and the guard gave her a grim look. He then said something completely unintelligible to her, and she stared at him.

A man—she thought the coachman—cursed. The guard shouted a reply, then looked back at her and let the step down.

"Oh, thank you—"

The guard snapped a retort and strode away. She had no idea what he said, except that she took by his tone that she had best hurry. She struggled to get down, clinging to her satchel and books, and her toe caught. She pitched face-first into a solid male chest.

She heard the *whoosh* of his breath as his hard arms locked around her, steadying her as her feet found purchase on the ground. For a moment she was dazed and felt the earth float away from her feet, but then she felt substance beneath her boots once more.

She drew in a difficult breath through the rough stuff of his coat and smelled wool and leather and wood smoke—a much better kind of scent than she had been forced to endure in the coach. She had the impression of a very large man, for he made her feel small and she was no small woman. She, her father had said, was built upon practical lines.

The man's arms loosened, and she leaned back.

"Oh, thank you, sir, I . . ." She paused and gazed up. The man staring down at her face looked so angry and forbidding that she choked off her words.

His hair was dark and pulled back in an archaic queue, he wore a common low-crowned hat, and dark bristle showed on his jaw and chin. His face was square, his brows thick and dark, and his skin swarthy from the sun. A simple neckerchief was knotted above his rough country coat collar; it appeared to have been tied there as a necessity, with careless efficiency and no thought to fashion.

Not that this was a fashionable gentleman. He was perhaps some country squire—and one not so very happy to have a full-grown woman flung into his arms.

She swallowed and spoke again. "I am so sorry." She pulled back, and his hands dropped away as if burned. "I—"

It was then she heard the coach. She whirled and saw it rolling—with her trunk lashed to the boot. "Oh, no! Stop! Stop! Someone please stop that coach!" She picked up her skirts and ran pell-mell after it, waving a hand, crying out. The coach gathered speed and surged out onto the narrow dirt road.

Cora stumbled to a stop, heaving for breath, staring after the coach in dismay. Then, despairing, she turned around.

The large countryman was standing there, watching her. She seized upon the chance.

"My trunk . . ." she said. Her voice came out weak and breathless. She tried again. "My luggage is on that coach." She paused, staring at the man. The man stared back. She realized that no one who heard her would care, and certainly the staring rustic would not.

Her eyes teared, and she was mortified. She never wept. But the lost trunk contained her most precious possessions in the world—Father's medical instruments and Father's journals.

The man suddenly bent and straightened with a satchel and a small bundle. Belatedly, she recognized her own things. In a surge of panic, she realized she could lose everything.

"Sir, those are my . . . things." She picked up her skirts and started boldly toward him, feeling as if she were approaching a wild boar or something worse, but she continued nevertheless. It was odd, but in her skewed frame of mind, her remaining possessions were worth her life.

"Sir, those are my things," came a high-pitched, mocking voice. An urchin skipped in front of her, grinning a gap-toothed smile. She stopped. Another urchin appeared on the other side of her, laughing, and snatched at her gown.

She wrenched back and heard the tearing of fabric. "Get away! Stop it!"

"That is enough. Go. *Now.*"

Cora jerked her gaze to the source of the voice— the very frigid, dark voice that reverberated up her backbone. She was in time to see the rustic stranger, now suddenly close, wearing an expression that could have frozen blood. The expression was not for her, however. It was focused toward the sound of rapidly retreating little feet.

He still held her satchel and books.

"Oh." She took a deep breath and let it go. This man had rescued her. She understood now. He wasn't a thief or a half-witted mute; he was being chivalrous, no matter how unwillingly. "Thank you, sir, again."

He looked at her. This time she noticed his eyes were very dark, the color of evening shadows.

"I am expecting someone," she said. Her cousin was to send someone to meet the coach, but what if she had been forgotten? What would she do in this godforsaken place? She spared a quick glance around. Beyond a pair of small stone cottages and a neglected stable, she saw endless fields rising and falling gently, cut by the path of a meandering stream. The sun was on its afternoon path. No one save the stranger was in sight.

"You are going to Wintercroft?"

She snapped her gaze to his harsh face. His speech was surprisingly understandable. "Yes."

"Then you are expecting me."

He turned with her things and began to walk. She had no choice but to follow. Even without her bags she had to hurry to keep up with his long strides. *How very peculiar this was. What an odd, curt, ill-mannered man.*

His rig proved to be the vintage dogcart on the far side of the stable yard, drawn by a beast of uncertain pedigree and age. No one attended the dogcart, but it was clear that the horse had no inclination to wander. It stood with head hanging low, one hind foot cocked and resting, with no sign of life save the twitch of an ear at a trespassing fly.

The man strode up to the cart and tossed her bags lightly in the back. Then he turned to her.

"Quickly, then."

"I beg your pardon, sir, but I have just lost my trunk—"

"We must hurry if we are to catch the coach before the crossroads."

Her heart leapt in hope.

"But, sir . . . surely with . . . this conveyance—"

She never completed her objection, for her cart driver seized her around her waist and, quick as a cat could wink, whisked her up and deposited her in the seat. In another blink of time, he was beside her, the reins in his hands. He gave a sharp command and slapped the reins against the beast's back. And the beast, which looked to be so much rawboned laziness, snapped to action. They rolled out of the inn yard at the speed of the beast's shambling trot, which proved to be reasonably rapid if not graceful.

It was also exceedingly uncomfortable. Cora had driven a dogcart herself, but never at more than a rapid walking pace on such a rutted road. At their present speed she felt as though she were bouncing down a stony hill on her bottom.

"Sir . . ." She clutched her bonnet to her head

with one hand, clung to the seat with the other, and managed to turn to view the driver's harsh profile. "Should we go more slowly?"

The cart hit a bump that snapped her teeth together, luckily missing her tongue.

"No," he barked.

Well, she thought. *Perhaps he believes I am a new kitchen maid. But Great-aunt's old lapdog was a great deal more polite.*

The mystery of the man's identity was rapidly becoming unimportant, however, for as she looked past the rollicking behind of the horse to the curve ahead, she saw she would need to grab hold with both hands. She only hoped that when she released her bonnet it would stay on her head. Her other hat was in her trunk, and who knew what would become of it?

"I think we—should slow down," she said. "I am not—cream, and I do not—need churning."

He answered her by guiding the horse off the road and then into the field.

"What! Are you deranged?" Cora cried, seizing the seat.

"Quite likely," he snapped. He slapped the reins on the horse's rump, and the horse lunged ahead through chest-high grass.

Cora's heart lurched in her throat and she considered the dire fate that might await her. There was some mistake. Surely this man was not Lord Wintercroft's man!

Moments passed and the Mad Cart Driver kept

urging the horse on. It occurred to Cora that he was in too much of a hurry to be seeking a secluded spot to have his way with her—he had simply chosen to drive through the field. This of course meant that she was still at risk of being thrown headlong to the ground.

"Where are you going?" she gasped at last.

"Where do you think I am going?" he answered.

"I cannot tell—your thoughts, but I am sure—that any place I wish—to go may be reached—by means of a road."

"Apparently you are wrong."

"I—" Here Cora lost her voice as the cart hit a tremendous bump. Quick as a cat, his hand was around her wrist.

"Hold tight!" he barked.

She felt a sickly flutter in the pit of her stomach. Breathless, bouncing, she caught sight of his large, gloved hand encompassing her wrist, and she felt the steely strength of it. But they were *not* slowing.

"I—am trying—to do so."

A bank rose before them. He released her wrist and took the reins in two hands once more. Cora held on for all she was worth, and they tipped up . . . and up . . . and skidded . . . and slowed. At the last possible moment, the homely horse gave one more mighty pull and the cart came up level upon the road.

Her rude driver turned the cart northward, and she saw a small collection of rustic buildings not so very distant. An inn.

He turned them expertly into the inn yard, brought them to a stop, and jumped down from the cart. Then he turned to her with outstretched arms.

"Come along."

"But I don't—"

"*Come.*"

Reluctantly, she allowed him to lift her down. Once upon the ground, she found it not as solid as she would have liked. It was as though she were a boat on water.

"There is the coach now. Follow me."

She heard the rumble and crunch of wheels on stone and looked up, but the world began to turn around her. Grasping the side of the cart, she bent her head down once more.

"The coach will not wait. Moreover, I have no desire to dangle about!"

"I am sorry," she whispered. She was not well. Not well at all. "I cannot come."

"I do not know which trunk is yours," he snapped.

He reached for her. And just as his hand slipped beneath her elbow, she lost her last meal upon his boots.

Chapter Two

He was silent, perfectly silent, for all of half a minute. Then he let out a great breath.

"You might have warned me you were ill," he said.

"I believed I had."

"Clearly you were much too subtle." He turned on his heel and began walking sturdily toward the carriage. Cora, who was yet wiping her mouth with her handkerchief, hastily dashed it to the ground and hurried after him. Since she was still somewhat dizzy, her course was not straight, but he did not turn back to see that.

"The coach will wait but another three minutes or so," he cast back to her. "Quickly, tell me which bags are yours, or you shall lose them for good."

He stopped by the coach, and she managed to catch up with him there.

"It is the large wood chest on the boot. And on top, the rattan box with the leather strap is mine—the larger one. And—and the small case just beside it."

He made a *harrumph* sound and turned to speak to the guard.

As soon as the first box was got down, Cora sat upon it, but all too soon the others were unloaded. She noticed her driver tip the guard, another thing that prompted a question in her mind. The driver was such an odd mixture of qualities, and together they did not form a man whose position and character she could identify. She wished to know more of him, and yet she could not dignify her cousin's employee by requesting a personal introduction. She determined she would do so as soon as the cart was loaded.

Her driver saw to the loading of her baggage in the dogcart. Cora waited and thought longingly of a drink, but was uneasy asking for one; surely it had to be purchased, for the only other was water from the well, which would be foul.

"Come. Let us start."

Cora accepted her driver's help into the cart, and then abruptly he strode away into the inn. She stared after him, and when a moment had passed, indignation flared in her breast. The very nerve of it! She was near fainting from want of a drink, and he went inside to refresh himself, leaving her sitting in the cart! She was in full view of the coach yard, too, on exhibition for travelers to stare at and speculate upon. It would serve him right if she were in a dead faint when he returned or was abducted in his absence!

She was prepared to have words with him, but when he returned, he carried a cup. Silently he came to the cart and handed it to her. He had surprised her again.

She drank gratefully, and uttered a quiet thank-you when she handed the cup back. He made no sign of acknowledging her, but turned wordlessly and took the cup back to the inn.

They were abruptly on their way again. This time the pace was not hectic as before. That did not stop her from feeling every bump in the road and observing to herself that there seemed to be a great many of them, but at least she could ride without fear for her life.

She took the opportunity to further study the man beside her, giving him furtive glances while she pretended to gaze about at the countryside.

He held himself very erect in the seat, she noticed. His movements were steady and purposeful to a fault; he could, she felt, remain entirely too still for a lengthy period of time, and she found this strangely disconcerting. Casting another glance his way, she took note of how large his hands seemed inside his snug-fitting gloves, and of how his shoulders appeared to rest like a hewn beam across the breadth of a sturdy house, steady and quietly strong. His poorly cut coat detracted somewhat, and also, she did not like the grim set of his mouth. But he did have, she decided, a rather nice profile if one could overlook the somewhat too forceful aspects of it. His was a face that would never be taken as belonging to a mild-mannered man.

"Do you find something to please, Miss MacLaren?" he asked.

Cora started. He continued to stare ahead at the road, and she quickly took her gaze from his face.

She raised her chin. "It is difficult to speak to someone who will not look at one. I should like to know by what name I may call you."

"You may call me Zander."

She was silent again for a time, angry that he had made her feel foolish with his impertinence. She decided he was the steward or some such and fancied he was a great deal more important than he was. Likely he was taking advantage of a feeble old man. That might even explain his unfriendliness toward her.

"Exactly what is your position at Wintercroft, Mr. Zander?"

"Essentially whatever I will it to be."

This was disturbing indeed.

"I do not find that amusing, Mr. Zander. You *are* from Wintercroft, are you not?"

He hesitated before answering this time.

"I am, Miss MacLaren."

She was still considering how to reply to him when he spoke again.

"We are arriving. If you look across the stream and up the rise you will see it."

Cora looked. Silhouetted against the sky was a cavernous hulk of stone with a large round stone tower rising on one end and a shorter, crumbling one on the other. All in all it was an eerie sight, for it had the look of being deserted. It was all very fine to be told that her cousin lived in an old stone pile; it was quite another to confront it.

"Can that be . . . ?"

"That is Wintercroft. Not what you expected, I would guess."

"I had no expectation whatsoever."

"I would not choose it for comfort, and one does have a tendency to catch chills in the place."

"Mr. Zander." She stared pointedly at him and at last he looked back. There was an oddly speculative look in his dark eyes.

"Mr. Zander, the reason for *my* choice is none of your affair."

He held her gaze. His eyes hooded slightly. "But at least the moat is drained," he said.

He directed the horse across a narrow old stone bridge, and then they began the steep approach to Wintercroft.

As they rattled and bumped up the narrow road, Cora had ample time to form an impression of it. Trees were sparse, she saw, giving the hill a barren and forbidding character. At the top of the hill, Wintercroft loomed closer, with its grim medieval visage and crumbling tower wing, and a lone gull circled above, oddly silent.

A picture of Lord Wintercroft grew in her mind. She saw an old, decrepit gentleman in a threadbare coat, hobbling slowly with aid of a cane. He would need such things as many elderly need: a good bath, proper grooming, and good food. It was likely he was receiving none of these things and just as likely that he did not want them; but she was accustomed to that. She had nursed a number of elderly patients, both before and after her father's death.

The wind brought with it the damp scent of the sea. The sea! She had never before visited the seaside. Her spirits lifted. She would take Lord Wintercroft walking there. In her mind's eye she saw herself walking with the old man, holding his arm, while he grew steadily stronger and the light came back to his eyes.

All of a sudden the cart came upon the crest of the hill. A field swept away from them, and beyond its distant edge appeared an endless stretch of blue. The grandeur of it gripped her, and she could almost understand why young men chose a life on the sea.

"Do you like the ocean, Miss MacLaren?"

The masculine voice reminded her of her driver, Zander. She had been nearly successful in forgetting him.

"I believe I shall."

She looked at him and found him gazing forward as she had last seen him, although she could have sworn she had felt his eyes on her an instant before.

"You reserve your opinion?"

"I always do. Most errors are due to a lack of consideration."

"And supposing you do not have all of the evidence? Do you never take a step?"

She hesitated and then said, "I am here. That should be answer enough."

"Indeed."

He said nothing more, and she found herself unsatisfied in spite of the nagging thought that she should not give a snap of her fingers for his opinion. But

Wintercroft loomed before them, and she was able to thrust aside her irritation to prepare for this new challenge.

The side of Wintercroft they approached was of sheer stone framing a very tall arched doorway, and it looked for all the world like the entrance to a medieval keep. It was in front of this door that the cart stopped. Zander jumped down, crossed to the door, and pulled on a thick, ancient-looking rope.

While she waited, Cora examined her surroundings. The drive was sunken and rutted; near to it were chunks of stone that had tumbled down from the wall—or the roof, as the case might be—and been left where they had fallen. Some sort of brambly bush grew in profusion along the wall and on either side of the door and appeared to stop short of the door by some will of its own, for no human hand was evident in its direction.

A damp chill pierced Cora's awareness and she pulled her shawl closer. Zander made a disdainful sound under his breath. He abandoned the rope and went to the great door, where he set upon unlatching it himself.

"Perhaps if you ring again," Cora said.

In answer, he hauled the door open. It swung back with a painful creak. Zander returned to the cart, jumped in, and took up the reins. The old horse, now in a pleasant doze, seemed not to notice.

"*Walk*, Caesar. *Forward*, you blessed bag of bones, or I'll tan your hide!"

Caesar apparently decided that he wished to comply and went shambling ahead through the stone archway and the short, vaulted corridor that followed. The cold air of the passageway made Cora shiver.

"Welcome to Wintercroft," Zander said.

There was no second door. The passage ended in a courtyard that was open to the elements. Straight ahead was a set of stone steps leading to a smaller door, apparently the entrance to the residential quarters. Zander brought her to the steps, stopped, jumped down, and in short order handed her out of the cart. He then preceded her up the steps and sounded the knocker loudly. Then he started back down the steps.

Cora turned toward his retreating figure in astonishment. "Where are you going?"

"You may let yourself in if no one comes," he tossed back.

"This is not proper. I cannot let myself in."

"I presume you cannot unload the cart and put up the horse. The door is a small matter."

He began to lift down her possessions from the cart, and Cora saw he would not be moved. Incensed and apprehensive, she turned to the door. She waited. She could hear her trunk landing on the cobbles behind her and finally the squeaking as he climbed into the cart. She stepped up to the door and opened the latch.

The door swung back with relative ease. She faced a cavernous hall, and with the light from slit windows high above she was able to gaze about herself.

She stood upon a stone floor worn smooth with the passage of centuries. On the wood-paneled walls hung an intimidating array of armaments, and centered in the room was a long, primitive wood table, dark with age and covered with ancient scars. On either side of the table were two long wood benches. There was nothing else.

Nothing, that was, except a choice of three doors. As she stood in contemplation, one of them opened.

In her fanciful imagination she expected a person in medieval garb carrying a flambeau. Instead she saw a young woman in deep mourning. The woman in black approached wordlessly, and as she neared Cora noticed an expression of somber resignation in her eyes.

"I am Cora MacLaren."

The young woman stopped before her, and her gaze quickly darted down and up, taking Cora in.

"What is your purpose?"

Cora blinked. A horrid possibility leapt to her mind. "Lord Wintercroft—is he well?"

The young woman's face did not alter in the slightest. "As well as ever. Why do you ask?"

"Because he has sent for me."

Silence. The woman continued to gaze at her, examining her, assessing her, questioning her.

"My coach was met," Cora went on, "by someone who calls himself Zander. I expect he will be bringing my things in shortly."

The young woman's brows rose slightly. "I see." She hesitated for a moment, her countenance betraying not a hint of expression.

She spoke again at last. "Then you must come in. You may follow me." She turned and started back toward the door by which she had come, and Cora followed.

Chapter Three

To Cora's relief, the surroundings became more customary once they passed through the inner door. She was now in a smaller hall with a parquet floor, carved wainscoting, and paneled walls. Between wall sconces, which were in severe need of cleaning, were several closed doors. At the far end of the hall was a stair.

The woman in black preceded Cora up the stair. On the next floor she walked to the last door and rapped.

Cora waited. There was no response. The young woman opened the latch and pushed the door slightly inward. Immediately an irate voice crackled from within.

"I didn't ask to be disturbed!"

"You have a guest," the young woman said. "A Miss MacLaren, whom you have been expecting."

"Who?" snapped the voice. "A guest? I'm not expecting anyone!"

The young woman in black pushed the door open

fully, moved aside and looked pointedly at Cora. Cora stepped into Lord Wintercroft's refuge.

Lord Wintercroft's study was cavernous and crowded with such things as a gentleman collects in a lifetime. An assortment of old swords hung above the mantel and there were also a Chinese lacquer chest, a fine mahogany cabinet holding goblets and several crystal carafes of liquor, and a surprisingly large jade elephant with several crumpled neckcloths dangling from his upraised trunk. Cora noted these things, and took in the dust and the cobwebs in the corners of the room in the moment before the door closed quietly behind her. By then her attention had gone to a gray-headed man who was hunched over the desk with his back to her. Over his bowed shoulders he wore a red coat; beyond that, she could tell little else.

She cleared her throat. "Good afternoon, Lord Wintercroft."

His head rose from whatever it was he studied in front of him. "What? Who is it? Who is in my study?"

"It is I, Miss—"

He turned abruptly, moving the chair and all, and fixed her in a fierce gaze. He surprised her into a start.

"—Miss Cora MacLaren," she finished.

His face was hard and craggy and his eyes as dark and piercing as a hawk's. His hair, grizzled and thick and too long for fashion, stood at odd ends and angles, as though he had run his fingers through it. But his coat, which she saw was of a fashion several seasons past, still fit him properly at the waist, and he wore it buttoned over breeches and immaculate hose. In addition, it had been brushed, and nary a speck of dust lay upon it.

"Who in bloody creation is Cora MacLaren?"

Cora blinked and stood gazing back at the cantankerous old gentleman—only he wasn't quite so old as she had supposed, and he was certainly no proper gentleman. He was past midlife for certain, and likely he had lived for more than a half century, but more than that she could not guess.

She did, however, note that his eyes had a particularly lively gleam. Her initial assessment of him was definitely changing.

"If you have forgotten your invitation to me, my lord, I am truly sorry. I have it in my pocket if you would like to see it. But if you have changed your mind you need do nothing but say so. I beg but one night's stay and assistance to return to—"

"Pah!" he snorted. He leaned back in his chair, reminding her of an old stallion who had got a scent on the wind. "An uppity wench at that! But what could be expected of a MacLaren! Damn wild Scotsmen! Bane of the family tree! Now I have one in my house! All thanks to an addle-witted female a century ago running off with one. Should have been locked up!"

Cora tilted her head inquiringly. "Do you mean your great-aunt Ermintrude MacLaren?"

Lord Wintercroft uttered another ungentlemanly epithet, which would have shocked a more protected young lady. Cora, however, had seen and heard enough of life not to be as stunned as—she supposed—he would have wished.

"I will not hear that female's name in my house!" He paused and drew breath, and appeared to be composing himself. However, Cora noted the glint of his eyes watching her from beneath his shaggy brows. "Never mind all that," he said in a testy, but calmer, voice. "Now that you are here I suppose I must see to you. Just like the rest of 'em, the beggarly rascals. There may as well be a MacLaren in the mix."

"The rest of them?"

He waved his hand. "Never mind, never mind." He fastened his gaze on her once more and then slowly stood.

Lord Wintercroft was taller than he had appeared while seated, and his shoulders appeared straighter as well. Only the thinness of his calves and the boniness of his hands gave his age away—those and the deeply etched lines in his face, which Cora felt could as well be from dissipation as age. She had the odd idea that he had intended to surprise her by pretending frailty when she entered the room. He would be pleased to know that he had succeeded.

He took a few steps closer and stopped when she began to be uncomfortable at their distance.

"Hm. Not much to look at," he concluded.

Cora, practiced in knowing her proper place and how to respond to her betters, suddenly found proprieties extremely taxing. This insult, combined with the method of her arrival, simply proved to be too much. She raised her chin. "If you had been all day in a coach, then driven by a madman from the coach stop home, you might find your appearance somewhat lacking as well."

He glared at her. She stared back. She did not blink, and neither did he. She realized then that unleashing her tongue might well cost her dearly.

Suddenly, he threw his head back and laughed. "Oh, my, oh, me! A madman! Oh, dear!" He withdrew a handkerchief from his pocket and wiped his eyes. "Excellent! Excellent."

Good Lord. Clearly Mr. Zander was not the only deranged person about. The other was her employer.

"Very well." He was abruptly sober again. "Take yourself to your chamber, then. Dinner is at seven, and I wait for no one. Since you are of a rustic background and a Scot, I suppose it behooves me to mention that proper attire is expected. That is all." He strode abruptly back to his desk and reached for the bell rope.

"Sir—"

"That is *all*, Miss MacLaren."

"I cannot dress for dinner. I have one good gown and I believe it may not do. Nor do I know if my trunk—"

"You shall have your trunk!" Lord Wintercroft snapped. "Stop nattering at me like a bedlamite!"

A scratching came at the door, and at Lord Wintercroft's command it opened to admit a thin, worried-looking maidservant.

"See to her," Lord Wintercroft barked.

"Y-yes, s-sir." She bobbed a quick curtsy, reminding Cora of a frightened rabbit, and then whirled on Cora with anxiety in her eyes.

"F-follow me, m-miss." The maid turned and darted off, leaving Cora and the open door to do as they would.

Cora followed, adding one nervous and stuttering maid to the company at Wintercroft. She began to fear that she might find herself to be the only resident who was sane.

She heard Lord Wintercroft muttering something about a wild Scotswoman as the door closed behind her.

Cora followed the nervous maid up two flights, watching her feet on the old stair, as the stone had worn down in the center of each step. At the top of the second flight Cora anticipated continuing up the third, narrower set of stairs, but the maid turned down the hallway toward the rear of the house instead.

This was the family floor, as evidenced by the silver candle sconces—black as they were—and the parquetry work on the paneled walls. It was not the floor upon which Cora would have expected to find her room. She wondered if the maid could possibly be nervous enough to make a mistake.

"Miss . . ." She had to repeat herself before the maid turned about with a startled look on her face.

"Mum?"

"Are you taking me to my room?"

"Yes, mum. It be this way."

Fancy that, Cora thought. She was being accommodated well enough. Perhaps, though, she was to take up residence in an adjoining chamber, where she would be convenient.

At the very end of the hall the little maid opened an oak-paneled door and pushed it inward. Backing into an awkward curtsy, she allowed Cora to pass and enter the room.

Cora stopped short and gazed about herself in wonder. The room was long and bright, as it featured two sets of French windows, both with drapes drawn back to let in the afternoon light. A large canopy bed reposed between them, its scarlet velvet drapes faded to rose. In the south corner was a rosewood writing desk; on the north wall was a wonderful hearth with an ornate marble frieze, and in front of it were a chaise and two armchairs. A door near the hearth was closed, but it clearly led to another chamber.

Cora stood still, turning her head to take in the minute details.

"Do you like it?" the maid asked, a little quaver in her voice. " 'Is lordship said it was t' be yours."

Cora looked at the girl, noting again the hint of fright in her eyes. "Of course I like it," Cora said. "I should be an ungrateful wretch *not* to like it. I only wonder if there has been a mistake. I cannot understand why Lord Wintercroft would put me into this room."

"He did say this were th' one," the girl said anxiously. "I know this is the room. I made sure of it."

Cora saw that the girl truly believed what she said. Cora would have to accept the room for now and make the best of it if the girl were in error.

"Very well, then. I thank you. I see my things have not been brought up yet, so I shall take a little walk."

It was the best action. She was abominably stiff from the awful carriage ride. When she returned, she would see if her bags had arrived in this room or another one.

"Should you not like refreshment? 'Is Lordship said I was to bring you tea."

Clearly, fear of " 'is lordship" was paralyzing the poor child. At least Cora assumed it was Lord Wintercroft the girl feared. Surely it could not be she! Cora gazed at her and decided to get to the root of the matter.

"What is your name?" Cora asked.

The girl dropped her head. "Birdie."

"Well, then, Birdie, I am sure that Lord Wintercroft wants my comfort," Cora said, while not certain of that at all. "I want nothing right now but to explore a bit and to have my things whenever it is convenient. You may go, reassured that I am perfectly satisfied, and I will be certain that Lord Wintercroft knows this."

Birdie bowed herself out, and Cora sighed heavily. Turning, she gazed at the giant canopy bed. In truth, she wanted nothing more than to throw herself upon it and sink into sweet oblivion—but she did not want to further wrinkle her dress when she had none other at hand, and she would not undress to her shift when that disagreeable Zander might appear at any moment with her trunks. Exploring was her only alternative.

Cora strolled to one of the windows and gazed

out. Before her eyes appeared the vision of an old
formal garden with precisely shaped flower beds, a
central fountain, and farther beyond those an exten-
sive pattern made up of tall hedges. It was hard to
make it all out from her vantage point, but if her
eyes did not deceive her, it was a maze. How intriguing! She had never before experienced a maze.

She was about to turn away when a movement
caught her eye. Below her appeared two figures, a
woman in black and a little boy.

It was the young woman who had greeted her,
for there surely could be no other young widow at
Wintercroft. The woman was slender and dignified
in bearing, and the boy, possibly five or six, scam-
pered ahead of her. She must have called to him, for
the boy looked back at her, then continued pell-mell
up the stone path to the fountain.

The fountain was large, with three marble nymphs
holding vases in the center, and a trickle fell from
each vase into the dark pool. The little boy stopped
at the walled edge of the pool, leaned over as far as
he could, and gazed within. The young widow had
picked up her pace and arrived shortly at his side.

Governess or mother? Cora watched a moment and
then decided she would have the answer from the
young woman herself. Cora lost no time, but was
soon upon the stair. Once she was on the ground
floor she would find the exit to the garden.

In conception, the matter was easy enough. But
when Cora reached the bottom of the stair she realized she no longer knew which way the garden lay.
For a moment she stood in the hall alone, then chose

a direction. With luck she would find the back of
the house.

Zander gazed at himself in his oval looking glass
and adjusted his cravat. Under normal circumstances
he would not fuss over such things. His style was
instinctive for the most part. But he was not precisely
a welcome guest, so certain concessions must be
made. Wintercroft was a stickler about dress.

*It would not hurt Wintercroft to be a stickler about a
few other things, as well.* Zander frowned at his waver-
ing image. *Amazing how the same man who dressed
down a dinner guest for a spot on his waistcoat could
allow a houseful of dust—and a houseful of a few other
things.*

But then, Zander thought, *Wintercroft had always
been a selfish man.* He attended to what was important
to him and ignored the things that were not. Dust
and tarnish he did not care about. Fashion and comfort he did—most of all, his own. The house could
be falling down so long as his dress was dapper, his
belly satisfied, and there was no leak dripping on his
head. And, oh, yes—Wintercroft also liked to be the
center of attention.

Unfortunately, that led to Zander's current un-
pleasant suspicion. Perhaps Wintercroft was not *ig-
noring* the current domestic situation.

Perhaps he was at the center of it.

Zander frowned. Wintercroft was a self-indulgent
pinch-purse, yet there were a number of reasons why
the house could be full of guests, all relatives with
nary a feather to fly with. All of the reasons required

Wintercroft's willing participation. And Wintercroft not only enjoyed being the center of attention—he enjoyed it most when it involved a devious game of his own making.

Now Wintercroft had added this girl, some sort of distant relative—and of all things, she was a MacLaren. Zander would have thought it impossible for the old man to allow a MacLaren into his home, let alone invite one. Just what was he up to now? She was neither particularly handsome nor exceptional in any way that Zander could see. Not in any way that might appeal to Wintercroft, that was. She had that fox red hair hidden beneath her bonnet, for instance. Hair that color was usually seen only in places where ladies didn't go; if it was natural, Zander could not tell. And needless to say, her clothing was plain and completely unflattering. One could hardly imagine Wintercroft being anything less than horrified at her appearance.

Zander himself found her to be courageous, at least, and determined. And lest he forget, possessing a pair of very fine green-gold eyes that seemed to have skewers shooting from them when they were aimed in his direction.

Zander's reflection showed a little smile pulling at the corner of his mouth. He removed it. He was here for a reason.

Profit? Perhaps no. Perhaps yes. It depended upon how one measured it. One thing was certain— Wintercroft did not intend to lose the game.

Zander carefully fastened his gold fob to his waistcoat. Suspended from it was the gold watch, polished to glittering perfection, that had belonged to his maternal grandfather. It was the only gold he wore, but it lent a distinctive air of respectability to his attire. Let Wintercroft try to fault *that*.

Zander shook out the lace at his cuffs and turned to face an evening of torment.

Lost. Cora frowned at yet another dusty, uninhabited salon, another in a long chain of dusty, uninhabited rooms. Underfoot were the remnants of a tapestry rug, chewed by mice and covered with bits of fallen plaster, and the walls she viewed wore draperies of cobwebs. An occasional patter and squeak from the walls told her the four-footed inhabitants lived there still, and were undoubtedly remarkably healthy.

She was in the unused portion of the old castle, not by design but by failure of her usually excellent sense of direction. What had begun as the seemingly simple task of finding a door to the formal garden had become a ridiculous exploration, replete with the smell of must and animal droppings, the remains of a dead bird, and the occasional broken chair.

It was a folly she could not afford. She was exhausted from the journey. She wanted rest. She cared not a whit now for a crumpled gown or for being seen in her shift by a dozen ill-mannered Zanders. In either case, she was so covered with dirt that she would frighten them all away.

She swept aside another cobweb and lifted the latch on yet another door.

It was a miracle. Before her was a newer hallway,

showing evidence of having been recently swept. She walked on, picking up her pace. In a short distance she discovered a narrow stair leading downward. And then in a trice, she was on the family floor where she had started her absurd adventure.

It was an easy matter to find her room, residing as it did in the rear right-hand corner. She opened her door and there, to her great relief, was her trunk and other baggage.

But that was not all. Something green lay across the coverlet of the canopy bed, shimmering softly in the slanting late-afternoon light. Bemused, Cora walked to the bed and lifted the lovely silk with both hands.

It was a gown—a beautifully worked, absolutely exquisite evening gown.

Chapter Four

Cora laid the gown upon the bed once more and cast a quizzical gaze about the room. Nothing else was unusual. Still mulling over the strange appearance of the lovely gown, she set about unpacking her things.

She had been about this for a quarter of an hour when a scratching came at the door. Cora, bent over her trunk, looked up. "Come in."

The door opened to reveal little Birdie and a water can that came above her knees. Birdie seized the handle with both hands and hobbled into the chamber with it.

"Your bath, mum." Birdie rested the can for a moment, then hefted it again and advanced four more steps.

Cora straightened. "Is there no one to help you?" The poor girl was so unmatched to her task that Cora was sorely tempted to lend assistance herself.

"No, mum, but I can do by meself. It a'nt hard." Birdie lifted the can once more. This time, shambling along rapidly, dangling the can awkwardly between her feet, she made it to the hipbath by the fireplace.

Cora dropped the shift she was holding back into the trunk.

"Thank you, Birdie. I shall manage the rest."

"Oh, no, mum. I am to pour it. And I am to help." Birdie stood still, her face mirroring exhaustion and worry. Cora was torn.

"Do you mean to help me with my bath, Birdie?"

"Yes, mum."

To someone who had always been the helper, the turnabout seemed strange, indeed. But something in Birdie's eyes told Cora that Birdie was desperately hoping that Cora would say yes.

"Very well."

The privileged treatment was a mystery, as much so as the arrival of the gown, and it troubled Cora. She knew the words of her great-aunt Leyburn's letter to Lord Wintercroft, and she could think of nothing in it that would have given the wrong impression as to her status. Soon enough the mystery would be mystery no longer, she supposed, but she now considered the possibility that there would be no need for her once matters were clear. It was not a comfortable feeling at all to be uncertain of her future.

Pragmatic matters rescued her from her brooding. Birdie, Cora learned, was a novice as a body servant. She had heart and the desire to please, but was in need of a good deal of instruction. It was necessary to tell her that to bathe one's back, she need not scrub it raw; and she needed to learn how to wash her hair without giving the floor an unneeded dousing.

Birdie took her instruction seriously. No matter how tactfully Cora corrected her, Birdie apologized profusely and promised never to make that mistake again. At last, while Cora sat at her dressing table and Birdie dried her hair, Cora came to the root of it.

Birdie was now toweling Cora's hair gently after her initial overzealousness. "You has be-ootiful hair, mum."

Cora smiled. Her hair had never been an advantage to her, ever attracting attention she did not want or need. For this reason she always kept it under a cap, where it rendered the least harm.

"Thank you, Birdie."

"You will look like a queen in that green gown. I just knows it."

Cora took a settling breath. "Birdie, the gown I am wearing to dinner is the one I have on the chaise longue, the gray one. It will need pressing."

Birdie's hands stopped on the towel.

"Mum? Ye'll not wear the green?"

"It is not mine, and likely it will not fit."

"But you will try it, mum?"

Cora sighed. "Birdie, that gown is for a lady in a much different position than mine. It would not be proper for me to wear it."

"But you are a lady, mum!"

To Cora's consternation, Birdie burst into tears.

"Birdie, what is it?" Cora turned to look at the maid, who had covered her face. Then she stood and took the girl by her shoulders. "You must stop weeping and tell me what this is about."

"I can't—"

"Yes, you can. Nothing will happen to you. I will not allow it. Now, calm yourself and let me hear what the matter is."

"I will never b-be a lady's maid!"

The ensuing tears came in a flood. Cora had to wait for the girl to stop sobbing to speak further, and this did not happen until she had Birdie seated in her chair with a glass of water to sip.

"Now, Birdie, is this all that is troubling you? That I do not wish to wear the gown? How could that possibly prevent you from being a lady's maid?"

" 'Is—'is lordship—wants you to—wear—"

"His lordship wants me to wear the gown?"

"Yes, mum."

"And if I do not?"

"He—he—he will let me go! And me ma an' the little 'uns will go hungry, 'cause I won't be washin' no p-p-pots no more!" Birdie hiccupped. "An' I want to maid you, mum. . . ."

Cora gazed into the tearful, pleading eyes of her would-be maid and felt her resolve weaken.

"I see." Indeed, Cora did see. There was a great deal more to Lord Wintercroft than a cross temperament. He was not above bullying his servants, and in all likelihood he would bully her, too.

However, Lord Wintercroft did not know Cora MacLaren. If it was a contest he wanted, he would surely discover what Cora MacLaren was made of!

ble "Very well," Cora said. "I shall wear the gown if it at all fits." *And then I shall have a little talk with Lord Wintercroft.*

Cora entered the dining room promptly on the hour of dinner, feeling not a little self-conscious in the green gown. Little Birdie had assisted her into it, as it would not have been possible for Cora to dress herself otherwise. The bodice was too small and too low for her abundant bosom, and her highly dressed hair served to give emphasis to this little fact. The only saving grace was that the dress was sufficiently long to cover Cora's worn black silk slippers.

Cora wore the only ornamentation she possessed other than her father's kilt pin—her mother's jade eardrops. The kilt pin had gleamed too defiantly at the center of her bosom, and she had decided that it had best remain in its box.

Birdie had marveled at her and told her how "be-ootiful" she looked, but Cora only hoped she was not *too* great a figure of fun. She had consented to wear the dress for Birdie's sake, but there were limits to her charity.

The moment the dining room doors were opened to her, she knew she had exceeded those limits.

Around the long formal table were seated no fewer than eight persons, and every face turned in her direction. For a moment the sound of a falling napkin could have been heard, if anyone had moved and inadvertently dropped one, but no one so much as blinked.

Cora stood frozen. Of the persons staring at her,

she recognized two—the woman in black and old Wintercroft himself. Cora averted her eyes, but not before she noted a mixture of expressions—surprise, shock, astonishment, and cool annoyance.

Lord Wintercroft, at the head of the table, cleared his throat and stood. Instantly there was the scraping of chairs as the gentlemen followed his lead.

"So you are here, Miss MacLaren," Wintercroft said loftily. "One minute late. But one time I can forgive." He motioned to a footman, who quickly hurried forward and pulled back the empty chair to Wintercroft's right.

Good Lord, I am to have the place of honor, no less. Is there no way to escape this outrageous exhibition?

It seemed very bad timing to claim illness and flee, although Cora did not think it impossible that she might momentarily become sick. Her father had always said that her one weakness was her nervous stomach, which had its way of choosing the most inopportune times to announce itself. She never flinched at blood or mayhem, oddly enough. She was affected only by bouncing carts, rolling boats, and silly situations such as these.

Cora drew a steadying breath and stepped forward to take her seat. *Oh, Lord, I wish I possessed a suitable shawl.* She considered the consequences of catching her toe in the beautiful green silk hem, but avoided that catastrophe and made it to the chair.

"Ah, very good, very good!" said Lord Wintercroft as the footman seated her. "Introductions are in order, for I am certain everyone is curious. Sit down, gentlemen! Sit!"

Cora did not look up as the men seated themselves. Instead she briefly composed herself and then raised her eyes to her host, who continued to hold forth at the head of the table. Cora noted that his gray hair was carefully combed, his dress was immaculate, and there was a particular glint in his eyes. She hesitated to look at the others, so her study of him was quite thorough.

"Let me introduce to you your cousin Miss Cora MacLaren," he said grandly, "a descendant of my great-aunt Ermintrude Neadow MacLaren." A sly smile came to his lips. Lord Wintercroft paused to gaze about the table, clearly enjoying the reaction to his words.

"An unfortunate orphan," he continued. "Once her situation came to my attention, I could not rest until I brought her into the bosom of my family. One must let bygones be bygones, don't you agree? I cannot blame her for her heritage, after all."

Cora felt the heat slowly rising to her cheeks, and they grew even warmer as Lord Wintercroft rested his eyes on her particular contribution to the family bosom. Incensed, she returned a level look, but he had already glanced away, his eyes traveling from face to face around the table.

"Of course, lingering on as I am, sinking ever more deeply into my dotage, I have need of comfort and balm for my sagging spirits. Miss MacLaren could not have prevailed upon me at a better time."

"That is nonsense" came a querulous female voice. "There is nothing wrong with your spirits. And I fail to see why you are in need of anyone when you have all of us."

"Misunderstood by my own dear sister! Eliza, I am injured to the quick."

Cora had to look up at this juncture. Eliza, a woman of fifty-odd years whose stout form was draped in deep purple bombazine, sat at the corner diagonally opposite Cora.

"I have said my piece," the older woman huffed. She sent a snappish look at Lord Wintercroft, but upon withdrawal she averted her gaze to meet Cora's for the briefest moment. The look skewered Cora with contempt and distrust.

Cora had no time to digest this affront. Lord Wintercroft was introducing her in his grand style, much as a man presenting a rare show for viewing. His sister's anger had affected him not at all—in fact, his amusement seemed increased.

"Miss MacLaren, my dear widowed sister, Mrs. Plymtree. Her son, by the by, Mr. Bertram Plymtree, sits at your right hand."

Cora lifted her eyes to the person next to her for the first time and met the limpid, pale gray eyes of a heavyset young man with a receding hairline. Bertram gave her the barest nod, his expression indicating polite disinterest.

"On my left hand you find Mrs. Robert Neadow and Mr. Robert Neadow, who have honored me with a visit. Robert is my late brother's son. And between my nephew Robert and my sister is Mrs. Arthur Neadow, my son's widow."

At last Cora knew the identity of the widow, along with the added bit of information that Lord Wintercroft had had a son. She wondered how long he had been deceased, as his wife was not more than perhaps two and twenty. She was again in black, but the gown was of silk tonight, trimmed with a fine black lace. Her dark hair was elegantly styled with no ornamentation, bringing to Cora's notice her very beautiful face. She did not return Cora's look, however, but sat as though Cora—or anyone else, for that matter—did not exist.

Of Mr. Robert Neadow and his wife Cora found nothing distinctive. Robert was an ordinary gentleman, thirtyish, neither handsome nor plain. His wife was light-haired, plump in an attractive way, and seemed very young. With her smooth pink skin and round eyes she appeared to belong in the schoolroom.

Lord Wintercroft was now introducing her side of the table, for there were two gentlemen yet unnamed seated to Mr. Bertram Plymtree's right.

"Mr. Roland Neadow, my brother's younger son, sits nearest the door. Roland is rusticating with us for . . . how long will it be?"

He answered in a cynical drawl. "I find I have not tired of the view as yet. In fact, it has just become more intriguing."

Cora could not see past Mr. Bertram Neadow, but she instantly knew that Roland was the dandyish dresser she had noticed when she entered, seated as he was at the corner of the table in easy view from the hall. She also knew that the "view" he referred to was herself. She felt her color rising again—since she was a redhead, this effect was never subtle.

"I am ashamed to call you nephew," Eliza Plymtree whispered sharply.

"Miss MacLaren," the nephew drawled again, "please accept my sincere apologies—and might I add that I am pleased at your acquaintance?"

"Enough," snapped Lord Wintercroft. "I am not done. I have yet to introduce the heir to the title, who dropped in upon us unawares this Thursday past."

For the first time, Lord Wintercroft's voice lost its flippant tone, and an edge of irritation crept in. Then he spoke again and the amusement was back, along with an undertone of eager anticipation.

"Miss MacLaren, between Mr. Roland Neadow and Mr. Bertram Plymtree you will find Mr. Alexander Neadow. But I believe an introduction is unnecessary. I think you have already met my son."

Son? Lord Wintercroft has a living son?

As luck would have it, Bertram chose that moment to lean back and withdraw his pocket watch. In that instant Cora met the dark-eyed gaze of the gentleman next to him and found her anxiety to be entirely justified.

Alexander Neadow was, of course, the infamous Zander.

Gone was the old-fashioned queue. Gone were the countrified coat and spotted kerchief. Alexander Neadow was clean-shaven, his hair was cut fashionably short, and his well-tailored blue coat fit him in a way the loose homespun coat certainly had not. Cora discerned all this in a trice, all the while the realiza-

tion that *this is Zander* causing a constant pain in her
temples—and in her stomach.

Yes, he was definitely Zander. It was Zander's rug-
ged face, as much as it had been tamed by the en-
hancements of a proper haircut, a shave, and an
application of soap and water. It was Zander's dark
brows and sun-darkened skin, and Zander's probing eyes.

Probing, but guarded. Assessing. Judgmental. Dark
blue gray, the color of a stormy sky. And as nonsen-
sical as it was, Cora felt a warmth suffuse her from
within that was quite different from how she expected to feel. This, and he had made a fool of her!

Alexander Neadow's eyes left hers and dipped
lower, then returned to her face with a subtlety of
expression that she immediately understood. It also
infuriated her. The warmth she experienced was now
blooming in her face.

"Ah, yes," Lord Wintercroft said cheerfully. "My
son is the gentleman who fetched you from the
coach. Or should I say the 'madman'?" He gave her
a crafty smile.

Cora found herself wordless. As there was no other
response, Lord Wintercroft continued.

"Yes, yes, my miscreant son, the madman, so pro-
claimed by a completely impartial stranger, so no one
can accuse me of unfairness. Not that she shall remain a stranger. Certainly not!"

Lord Wintercroft smiled again, this time at the
table as a whole. "Ahem! But who else have we here?
A nephew who never visits; a nephew who never
leaves; a nephew who clings to his mother and has

no views of his own. And then there is my dear unhappy daughter-in-law and my so deeply devoted sister who could not be compelled to leave my side. Do not look so, Eliza, or I shall believe you have put poison in my soup!"

"For shame, Augustus! Have you no sensibility whatsoever? To speak so of your own flesh and blood! And Joanna has given you a grandson, after all!" Eliza Neadow glared at her brother, her second chin trembling.

Cora spared a glance at the others. Bertram Plymtree did not appear to care. She had no idea what Alexander and Roland Neadow might look like, for she was not going to attempt to look at them; but of the rest, Robert Neadow was frowning, his wife was wide-eyed, and Joanna Neadow was as white as a ghost.

"I do not forget my grandson," Lord Wintercroft said. "Little Augie is my pride and joy. However, he is but five and a trial for my nerves. Allow me to continue." He cleared his throat and straightened his shoulders.

"My dear family, I have invited Miss MacLaren here so that she may make Wintercroft her home." He paused, gazing slowly about the table, an excited gleam in his eyes and surprising color in his craggy face. "But more than that—much more than that—I mean to make her my wife."

Chapter Five

T he silence lasted but a heartbeat and no longer. Cora, as much stunned as appalled, sat mute as the family gave voice to Lord Wintercroft's announcement all at once.

"Augustus, have you taken leave of your mind?"

"Uncle, can you have thought about this?"

"This is beyond anything! It is an outrage!"

Then, there was Roland.

"My, my. *Here* is a proper lark."

Eliza Plymtree turned her livid glare on her nephew. "Roland, I will have none of your sly tongue right now! Your uncle is an old fool, and *she* is no better than she should be! How can you joke about such a mésalliance?"

Roland, having the exceeding impropriety to appear amused, smiled back at his outraged aunt. "But he is *your brother*, dear aunt. I am powerless—a mere younger son of a younger son. I can hardly help it if he means to milk the pigeon."

"You might try, before he is past praying for! Bertram, what say you? Bertram? Bertram!"

Bertram, who sat silently with a vague expression on his face, started at his mother's command.

"Er—er—unusual. Yes. Indeed. Very unusual."

Eliza, thus exasperated by her own offspring, turned her furious gaze upon Cora.

"And what have *you* to say, Miss MacLaren? If indeed that *is* who you are!"

Cora, who had sat paralyzed through the squabble, had but one response at the ready—that she was as stunned as everyone else. But her lips had hardly parted when Lord Wintercroft broke in.

"Calm yourselves, dear ones. Calm yourselves! There is no need for all of this folderol. I wish to make myself happy. Can you have any objection to that? And as to my dear Roland's doubts of my abilities of the matrimonial kind, I might protest, but it is not of issue. I shall have companionship and she shall have a home. A perfect solution. I have hardly lost my mind." He hesitated, and Cora was to regret that she did not speak then and end the whole of it. But she did not.

"You see, there is nothing left for me but to begin once more. And in keeping with my decision"—Lord Wintercroft smiled again—"I mean to make my wife the sole recipient of my available fortune."

This time the storm of protest made the first seem the mildest breeze. Cora attempted to speak but was completely overpowered by the noise. If not for her ridiculous gown she might have stood on her chair and shouted out her refusal of Lord Wintercroft's supposed proposal, but as it was she feared she might need to duck a flying saltcellar.

Then Joanna abruptly rose, her pale face stricken, and rushed from the room. This had the effect that Cora had wished for but had been helpless to achieve. Silence fell swiftly over the table.

"What a pity," Lord Wintercroft said. "You have upset my dear daughter-in-law."

"*We* have upset her?" cried Eliza. "You have disinherited her son, while that—that woman is wearing *her gown!*"

Good Lord. Cora learned that she could indeed feel more mortified—something that had seemed an impossibility only a moment before. *Unbelievable! Intolerable! Outrageous!*

Lord Wintercroft had the grace to affect a look of regret. "Ah, 'tis so. But Miss MacLaren was in need of a dinner dress, and she does display it to perfection, do you not think?"

"This is quite enough!" Alexander Neadow slammed his hand on the table and came to his feet. It was the first he had spoken, and the effect upon the family circle was instantaneous. Silence was immediate. Judging from the pulse in his temple, Alexander was furious.

"You may misuse us all as you will. But I will *not* tolerate your abusing Joanna."

Lord Wintercroft's brows rose. There was nary a flicker of emotion on his face. "What? You, a hero for Joanna? I should not have expected it. But then, now that I will not be leaving my money to her son, perhaps she wins your sympathy."

"I do not care what you do with your blasted money. I *do* care that you have held her here on the expectation that you favored her son. If you were not my father, I would wish you to the devil."

"If you were my son, I should care for your opinion."

Alexander threw his chair back so vehemently that it toppled over and he slammed out of the room.

The silence now was unsettling. The exchange between father and son left Cora bewildered, but one thing was clear—there was no love lost between the two of them.

She took a settling breath. "This is absurd. I do not want any money."

There was no immediate response. Then Roland leaned forward and gave her a sly smile. "My dear, so you say now. But you will grow to like the idea quite well."

"Do not believe her!" cried Eliza. "One can see what she is!"

In an instant, the volley of words began again. Following the example of Joanna and Alexander Neadow, Cora rose and left the room. She could not get out of the horrid gown, or leave Wintercroft, fast enough.

Little Birdie was nowhere to be found. Cora cursed the luck that kept her in the green gown even a moment longer. Too disgusted to wait, and possessing the presence of mind not to tear a gown that was not her own, Cora looked for her shawl. Birdie had, of course, finished putting Cora's things away, and Cora at last found not her best gray shawl but her shabby old black one. Throwing this around her shoulders, she set about finding her way out of the house. She needed peace in order to think of a solution to her dilemma.

This time, being more angry than weary, Cora kept her wits about her and soon happened upon a back stair. She met no one upon the narrow, steep steps, for which she was grateful, and when she reached the bottom she found herself in a small back salon. There were doors both north and south, but praise heaven, there was also a set of French doors leading out of doors right before her.

Cora stepped out onto a flagstone patio flanked by a low balustrade. Beyond it was the park, the near portion of which had once been a garden but now had become overgrown. Cora followed the patio toward the rear corner of the dwelling where she supposed her room was located, watching for the parterre and fountain she had seen from her window.

Success! Quickening her pace, Cora rounded the corner of the patio and descended the stone steps into the side garden.

It was blissfully silent save for the distant call of a crow, seeming to claim ownership over the neglected shrubs and cracked stone. Cora did not mind. If the hedges were overgrown, she was cheered by bright yellow dandelions springing forth from the broken flagstone path; if the roses were choked with weeds, she was soothed by snowy clumps of oxeye daisy and the downy heads of purple knapweed. She passed ancient crab apples and overgrown honeysuckle, and was even caught by the bright purple and yellow flowers of the poisonous bittersweet climbing the stone wall bordering the garden.

The sun had nearly set and the sea wind blew cool. Cora tightened her shawl about herself.

Now, Cora, what sort of situation have you gotten into? She wandered down the path, retreating into her thoughts. *For the love of England, why does Lord Wintercroft want to marry me? And why did he not speak to me first? I cannot help but believe it was his intention to act exactly as he did. He is not at all what I expected. I believe he has brought me here under false pretenses.*

Lord Wintercroft seemed to be a very difficult man indeed—so very different from her own father, who had used his hands to help others until he was no longer able to leave his bed. Her father had given her that same passion to give aid and comfort.

And his son is as rude and bitter as his father is devious. As for the rest . . . I cannot worry about everyone, save my heart goes out to Joanna. What an unhappy situation for her.

How could it have been for Lord Wintercroft's sons? She thought about Alexander. In truth, the heir and surly cart driver had not left her mind, lurking in the shadowy corners even as she focused her thoughts on more practical matters. The man had played such a despicable trick on her, pretending to be of no account when he was Lord Wintercroft's son—even providing a misleading name! He knew his appearance at the dinner table properly dressed and groomed would shock her, and he had to have gleaned some perverse satisfaction from it.

Although perhaps I cannot blame him entirely for being such a rogue. I should not be surprised if Lord Wintercroft is largely at fault. But something else is wrong, too, between father and son.

Deep in her thoughts, Cora was upon the fountain before she noticed it. She stopped by its stone edge and gazed at the gentle fall of water, observing the murky turbulence in the green-black pool.

Destiny. It was such a thing as this, so dark and unknowable, while the turbulence of life made it even more obscure. One believed one had a plan, something that seemed faultless at concept. But then such unexpected things would happen. . . .

Her father's young death.

The compassion of a dying woman who insisted upon writing a letter.

An old man who decided to marry her, sight unseen.

A home so miserably lacking in caring and human kindness.

There were no answers in life. There was only hope in an unknown future.

What, then, should she do?

Cora was not one to run away, but neither was she a fool. If this situation was becoming a disaster, she had best seek another position. It was of course ridiculous to think of marrying Lord Wintercroft. No amount of material comfort could make the idea palatable in her mind. She was not wanted or needed here, and both Lord Wintercroft and the family would make her life a misery.

She walked slowly around the fountain, trailing her fingertips in the water. As she reached the far side, she saw something that made her pause—a message scrawled in charcoal.

On the stone, in a childish print, were the letters A-U-G-I-E.

Little Augustus Neadow—Joanna's son.

With her next heartbeat came a pang. His father was dead. He was trapped in this gloomy place, surrounded by grief and malcontent. Could he understand now how his grandfather tormented his mother over his own fate?

Cora hated the conclusion she was reaching—that there might be something here for her to do. How absurd! It was impossible!

She took her hand from the water and shook her fingers. No. Best to go and leave her unfortunate cousins to their own troubles. Her father had once told her that she could heal one person and feel fortunate, but she could never heal the world.

Cora sighed. This was her decision, then. She would leave. She felt a small sadness, but she pressed down the little voice that accused her of failure. She simply could not *fix* the Neadows.

She would start her life anew yet again. She would summon the strength to do so. Her path in life had not been an easy one, but few were. She could not wish for that which she was not meant to have.

At last her heart lifted. Her course was clear. She

would visit her old nurse in Yorkshire and write her inquiries for a position from there. Perhaps something might be available in Bath. She had always wished to stay in Bath.

It was coming on dusk now, and Cora was hungry, the missed dinner making itself felt. Still, the sight of the maze only steps away drew her. She stood and gazed at the ragged hedge before her, grown up tall and ominous like the wall to an ogre's castle.

She should go back. But perhaps she might take a peek—a very brief one, for the light was failing. It might well be her only chance before leaving Wintercroft.

With a sense of ease she had not felt in days, Cora stepped into the maze.

The maze, although overgrown, was passable. The box hedges towered above her head, and side branches reached out and brushed her as she passed. It was possible that no one had traversed the maze in years—the paths were laid with stone, and so no trace of human passage was left behind.

Cora walked on, holding the hated gown carefully so as not to tear it on the shrubbery. She went straight until she was forced to turn, and then she hesitated. But there was no possibility of her becoming confused; she could easily remember her own trail. She turned the corner and continued, and was soon lost in her thoughts once more.

"Find her! You wish me to go and *find* Miss Mac-Laren?"

Alex stood in a rigid posture, facing his father in the privacy of Lord Wintercroft's study. His answer was the aloof rise of his sire's right brow.

"I do not think I am difficult to understand. She is missing. Go and find her." His father, who sat in his comfortable chair before his desk, raised a glass of brandy and took a dainty sip.

Alex summoned all of his strength to withhold his mounting temper. The old man was pushing the boundaries of saintly patience!

"I see. Your bride-to-be has run off, and you have summoned me to go and retrieve her. Might I ask why you have not requested this delicate favor of one of the others?"

Lord Wintercroft leaned back in his chair and shuttered his eyes. "Why, it is because I know you are as close as a clam and allow nothing to pass your lips unless you determine it is in your own best interest. Quite naturally, you may not believe my upcoming nuptials are in your best interest, but you likewise know that you do not have a better option to choose. You know that I shall not favor you no matter I marry or not. That being the case, you may wish to examine my current choice more closely before suggesting to the others that there may be a weakness in my plan." He paused, and a sly smile came to his lips. "Of course, there is no weakness. No woman will refuse marriage to a fortune. And perhaps, after all, there may be something to be gained by having Miss MacLaren as your stepmother."

Alex bit down even more tightly on his rebellious tongue and dove deep into his store of cunning. "And perhaps I support your favoring Joanna's son."

His father's response was a loud snort. "Pah! That means nothing to you. You cannot marry her—she is your sister-in-law. Neither shall I appoint you Augie's guardian. And I certainly do not believe you have any real compassion for your brother's widow, since she so readily passed you over when she had the choice! But then, I do not believe you have compassion for anyone save yourself. It is an odd sort of strength, I suppose."

Alex's father was the one man who could goad him to the point of losing control. Alex knew this, and grasped at his mantra of strength: *Do not let him win. Be stronger than he is. Do not let him win.* But for the spark of a moment, his father's words made him remember all he wished to forget.

It had begun one clear summer day when his father had come home from London, bringing with him several couples that he liked to impress and amuse. Alex, who tended to keep to himself and ignore his father's entertainments, went hunting when the guests arrived. Also, given that his father's favorite was Alex's younger brother, Arthur, Alex knew he had nothing to lose.

He learned his mistake later.

When he returned, wearing his comfortable old hunting clothes and carrying a bag of grouse, he unexpectedly encountered the party admiring the medieval architecture in the old part of the hall. In the group was the most beautiful young woman he had ever seen—with his handsome young brother, Arthur, smiling at her side.

Alex had quickly repaired to his room to make himself presentable. He had not escaped the young woman's eye or the look of distaste that had come over her face at his careless appearance. Even more, Arthur had always possessed the fashionable slenderness, the face, and the charm that Alex lacked. But Alex was the heir, and as much as he hated making use of that advantage, it was the one he counted upon. For the first time in his lonely life, he was inexplicably, completely, in love.

Alex soon learned that his father had brought beautiful young Joanna Sterling and her parents to Wintercroft with a particular plan in mind. The Sterlings were new acquaintances of old name and stature. Joanna would have been the belle of the season if not for one thing: the Sterlings were not a well-to-do family.

That evening at dinner, his father had jovially announced that he would leave his fortune to whichever son won the heart of lovely Miss Sterling—and that Miss Sterling had one week to make her decision.

His father had crushed hope in him that night. Anger was all that sustained him—anger at his deceased mother for his questionable parentage, but most of all at his father, who delighted in this revenge on an unloved son. Alex could only hope that the beauty might learn what Arthur so readily kept hidden. Arthur was fond of women and drink and gaming, having been fussed and fawned over by a doting father since his arrival in the world.

But one week was more than enough time for Arthur to charm the beautiful Joanna, and not nearly enough for her to know him.

Alex found his strength and crushed the memory into the darkest recess of his mind.

"You may be wrong about my concern for Joanna's welfare," he told his father.

"It makes no matter whether I am or not. You will consider carefully before you decide to reveal Miss MacLaren's disappearance to all and sundry."

"Then you admit you are also at a disadvantage no matter which option *you* choose. In desiring me as your agent you have also placed yourself in my power. It must rankle you to no end."

Lord Wintercroft sat bolt upright, his attitude of sophisticated shrewdness lost, his face reddening with rage. "Devil! I always knew you were the spawn of Beelzebub himself! That is the reason you live while Arthur is dead! You likely arranged it all!"

Alex was silent for a moment as the familiar pain seared through his breast. He had long since learned to absorb it, to immobilize his face, to give away nothing.

"Be that as it may, I am the one you trust," Alex said.

"I do not trust you. I should rather trust a snake! But I do know you. Therefore, you shall go and find Miss MacLaren, and that shall be an end to it."

Lord Wintercroft turned abruptly back to his desk, dismissing Alex. Alex regarded his father's turned back briefly, and then spoke.

"Very well, I shall. But I should not suppose there is an end to anything if I were you."

Lord Wintercroft bellowed something after him, but Alex took great satisfaction in slamming the study door on the words.

He immediately encountered Joanna, who, judging by her loss of color, had been deliberately listening at the door.

She drew back a step, evincing some confusion. "I was just on my way to my chamber."

Alex gazed into her beautiful dark eyes and felt his anger drain away. It was always thus. He could not be angry with the woman who was as much a victim of his father as he himself was.

"It does not matter. I shall tell you anyway. My father has asked me to look for Miss MacLaren. Apparently she is not to be found."

Joanna bowed her head briefly and then looked up. "I believe I . . . I know where she is."

Alex continued to gaze at her. "Yes?"

Joanna took a breath. "I saw her go into the maze."

Alex felt relief, and at the same time a smile tugged at the corner of his lips. He would not, however, give it expression. "Indeed? And you have told no one else?"

She shook her head, her sad eyes filled with guilt.

"Thank you for informing me. I am very appreciative, Joanna."

Indeed, he was. Not only would his task be considerably easier, but also Joanna had allowed Miss MacLaren to be safely put in her place. He only regretted that Joanna would suffer for it.

Chapter Six

*I*t was twilight, but even darker in the maze. Cora's relentless thoughts had distracted her, and somewhere she had made a turn that she did not recall. She sat on a stone bench, deeming it useless to continue wandering about while darkness was falling.

Cora might have been afraid, but she rarely was. Instead she was disgusted with herself. She doubted anyone knew where she was, and if they did she did not believe they would come to rescue her. There would be no danger in the maze. There was only too much time for more reflection and a good deal of shivering as the night grew cool.

Some time had passed when she heard the sound.

At first she believed it was the sound of the gentle sway of tree branches in the wind. Next, she suspected an animal creeping through the thicket. The sound paused, and then there it was again—closer than before. It was the sound of stealthy footsteps on the damp earth.

It came from somewhere within the maze.

Cora parted her lips to call out, then hesitated. She continued to listen. The steps continued on their slow, quiet course, and all else was silent. She could not know who it was—and if it were anyone with her welfare at heart, he would call her name aloud. No, it seemed to be someone who had no interest in finding anyone, or in being found.

A chill crept over her that had nothing to do with the cool evening air. What next in this bedeviled place? A thief? A murderer? Not a very *clever* one to be skulking about in a maze, to be sure.

She was becoming silly from weariness and hunger. There was nothing amusing about some unknown person creeping about the maze. As much as she wished to escape it, she kept very still and listened while the measured steps came closer . . . closer . . . and passed her by on the opposite side of the hedge by which she was sitting.

Cora waited until the steps completely faded away before she drew a full breath. There—she had probably missed her only chance at escaping this despicable place! She was cold and hungry, and from time to time she slapped an insect from her face or a spider from her arm. She should have followed the intruder, as he likely knew the way out. Now she would probably need to sleep here, and would die of cold before morning in this ridiculous gown.

She did not know how much time passed as she waited. She sat on the bench until her bottom hurt, then rose and walked up and down, and then sat upon the bench again. It was darker now and the maze was quite black, although she could gaze up at the paler shade of the sky.

She was just wishing for *anything* to end her deadly boredom when she heard steps again.

"Miss MacLaren! Miss MacLaren, are you in here?"

At the masculine voice her heart shouted in relief before she could open her cold lips. "Yes, I am!" she cried.

"Keep talking, Miss MacLaren, and do not move."

"Might I attract some wild beast, that I must sit still?"

"I am coming to you, and I do not wish to be chasing you about this madman's forest all night."

Ah. She knew who her rescuer was now, although she had suspected his identity. That deeply sonorous and brusque voice belonged to Mr. Alexander Neadow.

"You need not worry. I am frozen quite stiff. It is a wonder I can speak."

"Yes, the world seems populated with wonders today."

She inhaled sharply in indignation. "Yourself chief among them, it would seem. I have never seen such a rapid promotion from the vulgar to the noble."

"We have something in common, then."

"You speak too soon on my behalf."

"It is good that you believe so."

Cora heard his step quite nearby and looked in the direction of the sound. There was nothing to see but darkness, but then she noticed a spot of white where she supposed his neckcloth to be. The spot of white bobbed rhythmically with his steps and grew larger as the distance closed between them.

"Where is your light, Mr. Neadow?"

"Your future husband forbids the waste of candles, Miss MacLaren."

Cora was not satisfied with that answer, but for the moment she was grateful to be rescued, even by a rescuer who was little inclined to do so.

She rose to her feet. He stopped in front of her. His head was a black form against the paler night sky, and she gazed up at his hidden face.

"Was this a mission of mercy or a mission of duty?" she asked.

"Neither." Typically, he did not elaborate, leaving her wondering about his meaning.

"You are very enigmatic, sir. I must wonder what you are about. Perhaps I shall call you Zander after all. He was easier to comprehend."

"Please do not. It is a name I prefer to be forgotten."

I should feel afraid, but I do not. However can this be? Cora stood facing her inscrutable opponent. As cold as she was in the ridiculous gown, a warm tingle started deep within and crept up her spine. *I am cold and warm at the same time,* she mused. *That is impossible, and yet it is true.*

The breeze stirred, and on it came a whiff of his cologne, something subtle and foreign like an oriental spice. The brush of air made her shiver.

Wordlessly, he slipped out of his jacket and without ado draped it over her shoulders. She felt its sudden weight, enfolding her in his warmth, and the soft, exotic scent rose about her and enveloped her.

I cannot deny this feeling. I am attracted to him. I must truly have lost my senses.

She struggled to find words to break the spell. "Then why did you call yourself Zander, if you wish it to be forgotten?" she asked.

She expected him to be evasive, but for once he was not.

"It was the first thought I had. It was the name my brother used for me." He took her elbow, and they began to walk. "It was a very long time ago."

"That leaves 'Mr. Neadow,' and as you have two cousins here of that name it is very confusing. I shall need to call you Mr. Alexander, Mr. Robert, and Mr. Roland."

"Perhaps you may. But perhaps it may not come to that."

"You do not like me very much, I think."

"My opinion is not personal, Miss MacLaren."

"At least you believe I *am* Miss MacLaren."

"Do not delude yourself. I call you Miss MacLaren out of courtesy only. Unless it is proven, to me you could be anyone."

"How can that be?" She stumbled and caught herself with the aid of his sturdy hold on her arm.

"I make certain of things, Miss MacLaren. When my father invites an unknown young woman to his household, I discover who she is. I have not had time to investigate your case as yet, but you may be assured that I will."

"You have not seen my great-aunt's letter," she said with heat. "She clearly explains who I am."

"In fact, I did see the letter. But one must wonder if you misrepresented yourself to Mrs. Leyburn, or if you are not the young lady on whose behalf she wrote to my father. Consider yourself warned, Miss MacLaren."

"I dislike your inference, Mr. Alexander."

"I am honest, which is more than you will have from the rest. In any case, it is about more than who you are. It is also about *what* you are."

"I beg your pardon!"

Cora stopped, forcing him to stop with her. She stared at his deeply shadowed face, not making it out, knowing he could not see hers. She could not remember feeling so angry.

"It is no mystery" came his mocking voice. "Impoverished women are always attracted to gentlemen of means. Particularly when the lady's inducements are few, an older gentleman is satisfactory, as long as the reward is sufficient."

"How *dare* you!" Cora fought the anger, struggling for the self-control she needed. She had never been accused of being dishonorable in all her life!

"I do not lie! And I did not come here intending to induce your father to marry me!"

For a moment he was silent. She could feel his eyes upon her in the dark. And then he leaned closer . . .

Startled, Cora pulled back, but was held in place by his powerful grip on her arm. She tugged frantically, feeling the hedge prickling at her back and the brush of his breath on her face. He grasped her other arm and pulled her to him, and in the next moment he slipped the coat from her shoulders and wrapped his powerful arms around her.

He was trying to kiss her. Good Lord! Cora struggled as if a wild creature in a snare, fighting against bonds that would not weaken, twisting her face madly from side to side to thwart his intent. But it was all for naught. He moved one hand to the back of her head, cupped it tightly, and crushed his mouth over hers.

When she realized he was forcing her mouth open, her panic doubled, but she was already struggling with every bit of strength she possessed. Then he stopped. He raised his head, stared down at her face, and released her.

Cora took one step back and slapped him hard. She slapped him so hard her hand smarted. Unfortunately, she caught him somewhere on the shoulder.

He moved back, placing a safe distance between them.

"You are being foolish, Miss MacLaren. I suggest you restrain yourself."

She drew a furious breath. "*I* restrain myself? *I*? I am not foolish, and neither are you! How *dare* you touch your *future stepmother*?"

"Perhaps," he said quietly, "it is because she is no more a lady than I am a gentleman." He stood silently, hands at his sides, watching her in the dark.

Hugging herself in the cool night air, she clenched her fists, hating the swell of tears behind her eyelids. *The devil take him. I will not cry. I shall prove him wrong—and make him take back every word.*

He waited and, when she did not respond, bent down, picked up his coat from the grass, and lightly slipped it around her shoulders once more. "I am trying to save you a great deal of difficulty," he said soberly. "You shall not last here above a fortnight. Your chances of becoming my stepmother are no better than those of becoming my wife."

Cora inhaled sharply. The wild Scotswoman within her rose with sword brandished.

"*Your* wife? When horses *fly*, sirrah!" She flung the words at him with all the frustration and fury that swelled within her.

He paused. If he felt the extent of her anger, he showed no reaction to it. "Just so," he said. "When horses fly. Shall we continue?"

She did not answer. He took her arm, and by unspoken consent they traversed the rest of the maze in silence.

Alexander knew that if Miss MacLaren's hand had struck his cheek, he would have been wearing the mark for a long time. She had surprised him, but he did not in the least blame her. He had deserved that slap. He had tried very hard to.

They had parted ways downstairs, and she had ascended the stair like a vanquished queen in her bedraggled finery, defeated but not humbled.

It disturbed him how attractive he found her.

Alex rolled angrily to his opposite side, then rose and punched his pillow. Relaxing once more in his bed, the cooling night air from his open window brushing over his skin, he frowned into the dark.

He had learned one thing about Miss MacLaren at dinner that he had not previously realized. In an old dress, shapeless cape, and battered bonnet, much about Miss MacLaren was hidden. But in a low-cut gown that was made too small, all came to light. Miss MacLaren was blessed with a form that would make Venus envious.

This made her even more dangerous. He had to keep a cool head—particularly if she proved to have a penchant for wandering about. Yes, Miss MacLaren would bear watching. He would simply have to refrain from enjoying it too much.

But with any luck, she would not stay. She was a fool if she did not see that her life would be made a misery at Wintercroft. She would need to be very desperate to stay—or be the very sort of calculating piece he had suspected her to be.

She would be just the sort who might learn too much . . . and just the sort of complication he did not need.

But at least he had learned the sort she was *not*. Miss MacLaren had no practice whatever in the art of seduction. Very likely, he had succeeded in making her hate him forever.

This was probably a very good thing, but the thought kept him awake until he heard the birds begin to stir.

The green gown was in very sad condition. Holding it out in front of her, Cora gazed at it ruefully while Birdie looked on. "I wonder if it can be put to rights," Cora said, half to herself.

"I don't know, mum."

The gown was wrinkled, the hem badly stained, and there were two small tears where protruding branches had done their work. Cora felt terrible. In her entire lifetime, she could not save enough to replace this gown.

"See what can be done, Birdie. I shall have to speak to Mrs. Neadow."

Birdie's eyes were very wide. Cora had no doubt that some of the events of the previous evening had come to the servants' ears, and the very idea of Cora speaking with Joanna Neadow would stir anticipation.

But first Cora needed to speak with Lord Wintercroft. It was time for his misconceptions to be corrected.

She found him in his study, perusing a book of plays. He looked up with alacrity when she entered.

"My dear Miss MacLaren!" he said grandly, rising to his feet. "Please be seated. I have been expecting you sometime or other. Although I do not know why you thought you would find me in the maze."

Cora took a seat near his, and he sat once more, relaxing with complete ease.

"I suppose you wish to know how you will be settled," he said.

Cora fixed him with a look of cool composure. "I wish to know how you came to consider us to be engaged without first asking me to marry you."

His brows rose. "So you think that way, do you? Would you have declined?"

"Yes."

He stared at her a moment, then smiled. "I do not believe you. My dear, you are not stupid, and you are poor. You have run through your near relations—nursed them to death, I understand—and come to me. You must not take it badly that I do not wish to have you nursing *me*. I wish to live a rather longer life. However, in a fit of generosity, I decided to marry you. I cannot see the objection to it."

"Perhaps I can help you, sir. On first meeting me, you made certain references to a portion of my family as being the 'bane of the family tree.' "

"I am afraid I was out of sorts. My great-aunt's behavior was a family embarrassment. You must not mind what I said, my dear."

"Then you said that I was 'not much to look at.' "

"No! I could not have done." His look of surprise was very credible. However, as the expression Cora returned was entirely skeptical, he amended himself.

"Although I do believe you were wearing that same beastly gown then as you do now. Your bonnet appeared to have been through a mill and you were covered with dust. You must be reasonable."

"I believe you expected a pretty girl from Mrs. Leyburn's letter and were disappointed in me. However, when I appeared at dinner in Joanna's gown, you were happy to continue with your plan."

"Plan? Pray, what plan? It is all generosity on my part."

"As near as I can determine, it concerns distressing the family."

"Poppycock!"

"And you have chosen me as the rod of punishment."

"My girl, that is quite enough! Have a mind to whom you are speaking! I will not have an ungrateful . . ."

He paused in midtirade, seeming to notice Cora sitting calmly, regarding him with an expression completely untouched by his display of outrage.

"Miss MacLaren," he began again, "what is it that you want? Some promise of everlasting affection? Well, you won't have it. And I shall not engage in a discussion of my motives. I require my wife to obey me as husband. You will have a roof over your head and some decent clothes, and *that* is all. Take it or leave it."

"I should prefer to go." She stood. "I shall need some conveyance, as I cannot afford one."

He stared at her, his face red with outrage.

"I wish to return to Yorkshire."

"Then *go!*"

Cora turned without a word and walked toward the door.

"Wait!"

She paused and turned around. "Yes?"

"You cannot mean to leave here with nothing. You have no position. No other family."

"I do what I must."

"I cannot allow it."

Beneath her cool exterior Cora's heart was beating hard. All depended on her next words.

"If you wish me to stay, you must respect me and

my wishes. I am not a potted plant to be left to wither and die."

He relaxed all at once, and an amused smile twitched at the corners of his lips. "Spitfire," he said. "So you wish to marry me after all."

"I have conditions."

"My dear Miss MacLaren, please sit. Then we may talk all about it. I am an old man, and I forget the passion of youth. Do you wish pretty words? I can say a few."

Cora returned to her chair. "I wish to be useful."

Wintercroft raised a brow. "Useful? In what way?"

"In any way that I may be. I have many skills, Lord Wintercroft. I am an excellent housekeeper. I am very good at organization and in making improvements. And I know how to economize."

"Very good. You will be able to keep busy."

"You must not interfere. And you must allow me the funds to accomplish what needs to be done."

"Within reason."

"I must be the judge of that. And I insist on a long engagement so that I may be assured that you will keep your word."

"Not a very trusting young lady, are you? How long do you wish our engagement to last?"

"Six months."

"Too long. I shall allow two months."

"Four."

"That determined, are you? Well, I believe I can accommodate you. However, I have a few rules of my own. First, you must get rid of that atrocious dress and allow me to purchase you suitable gowns. I shall send to—"

"Excuse me, sir, but I shall *not* wear anything similar to that green gown again. And I must have practical clothing."

"You may have practical gowns, of course. But you must be able to dress suitably for your position and for the occasional social engagement. I do not wish it thought that I am wed to a parlor maid."

"And I do not wish it thought that you are wed to a trollop."

"As you wish," he said impatiently. "To begin with, I shall send you to the dressmaker in town. She doesn't have much to offer, but it is a start."

"Joanna's gown must be replaced."

"She would never have worn it again. Do not concern yourself."

"I choose to concern myself. I wish it to be replaced."

Cora locked eyes with Lord Wintercroft for a moment, then he relented.

"Very well. I shall purchase Joanna a gown as well. As for my last rule, Miss MacLaren—you shall not intrude upon my business. You shall mind your own, not mine. Is that understood?"

Cora gazed at him for a moment, and then she smiled. "If you have understood *my* conditions, sir, then I understand yours."

When Cora left Lord Wintercroft's study, she was trembling with nervous exhaustion, even as her heart sung with victory. *I have done it.* Lord Wintercroft had accepted her on her own terms—and had subtly given her the upper hand. Oh, he did not realize it yet, but he had lost the moment he called her back from the door.

He needed her too much to let her go. She might be intended as an instrument of torment for his family, but *she* would be the one wielding the instrument. Things were going to change.

As for Mr. Alexander, she owed him her gratitude. Without his insulting behavior, she might be on her way. But he had made her see the error of retreat.

Miss MacLaren had a mission, and a certain detestable gentleman would not drive her away.

Chapter Seven

*I*t did not surprise Cora to learn that Lord Wintercroft possessed a conveyance other than the one-horse dogcart and a driver other than Mr. Alexander. The carriage was a landaulet, and the driver was a man called Will, the cook's brother, according to Birdie, who was to accompany Cora on her foray to East Dean.

East Dean was the nearest village, some two miles south along the coast and inland of Birling Gap and the place where the capable seamstress Mrs. Proud was to be found. Cora and Birdie set off the same morning Cora spoke to Lord Wintercroft—at his insistence. Cora reluctantly agreed, postponing her walk to the cliff for another day.

Birdie was very happy to go and chatted happily, raising her voice over the noise of the carriage wheels. She told Cora that she had grown up in East Dean, that her mother and brothers and sisters lived there, that her eldest sister had married a sailor, that he was now at sea and her sister was expecting. She also knew where to find the seamstress and told Cora that Mrs. Proud sewed gowns for Mrs. Joanna as well.

Cora was not so interested in the prospect of planning a gown as she was in seeing more of the Sussex coast. The road cut back away from the sea at Birling Gap, however, without passing close enough to the cliffs for much of a view, but the inlet at Birling Gap was picturesque, and inland she found the rolling grassland with its many strange wildflowers appealing. It was a sunny day and the sky was an endless blue. Cora felt at peace for the first time since her arrival at Wintercroft.

Birdie chattered on, conveying to Cora in one breath that her mother kept house for the vicar, her father had died at sea, and Birdie helped to support her six younger siblings with her pay.

Birdie earned her pittance, too, Cora thought. Cora had learned that Birdie was yet expected to fulfill her duties in the kitchen as well as be Cora's personal maid. Fortunately, Cora did not require much in the way of personal service, but she did not like to see servants overworked and the house filled with dust, cobwebs, and unmended linens. Staffing at Wintercroft was one thing she planned on improving.

"Look there," Birdie called out over the noise, pointing. "It is the biggest farm here. Me brother Sam helps with the hens."

The carriage continued from a rise downward, and Cora peered out her window to glimpse what lay ahead. On the approach they passed several fine homes, which were a pleasant surprise, before rolling into East Dean proper.

East Dean itself was small and old, nestled in a hollow. Neat whitewashed cottages ringed the village green, with a medieval church among them.

"It is a pretty village," Cora said.

Birdie smiled with pride and pointed again. "There is Mrs. Proud's."

When they got down from the carriage Cora saw a sign depicting a tiger suspended from the public house some way down the street. The town seemed a quiet little place, but she heard conversation and laughter coming from the open door to the pub.

"We shall not be long," Cora called to Will. She turned toward the little whitewashed cottage that was Mrs. Proud's residence and rapped on the open door.

A tall, slightly stooped woman rose from her seat in the shadowy interior and came to the doorway. She wore a raggedy shawl, and her black hair was pulled into a severe knot at the back of her head. Her face was pale and unlined, although Cora guessed she would not see forty again.

"I am Miss MacLaren from Wintercroft. I should like to have several gowns made."

Mrs. Proud nodded expressionlessly and motioned them inside. "I shall oblige as I can."

She indicated a chair by the fire, and Cora seated herself. Mrs. Proud turned to a sizeable wood trunk by the wall and opened it.

"What are ye thinking of having?"

"Two day dresses and one suitable for dinner, as

well as a new dress for my maid, Birdie. Lord Wintercroft will also purchase a new dinner gown for Mrs. Joanna Neadow."

The seamstress, bent over her trunk, peered back at Cora over her shoulder.

"The first three gowns are for yourself?" There was nothing in the question itself, but her tone probed for more.

"Yes. I am newly living at Wintercroft. I am a cousin to his lordship."

Mrs. Proud turned back to her trunk and began lifting out bolts of fabric. Out came a pretty sprigged muslin, a blue striped cambric, and a shimmery green silk.

"Not green, if you please."

Mrs. Proud replaced the green.

Cora gazed curiously around the cottage while Mrs. Proud chose more bolts of cloth. It was small and sparsely furnished, but there was a large square table in the center of the room covered with evidence of Mrs. Proud's trade—three gowns in varied stages of completion, one of black crepe, one of a figured turkey red, and one of a lovely yellow silk with a net overskirt.

"You say you are a cousin?" Mrs. Proud asked. "And 'is lordship is buying these gowns?"

"Yes. He is being very kind to me."

She was soon to figure in the town gossip, Cora thought. She looked over her shoulder to see if Birdie was listening, and was surprised to see that the girl had vanished.

"Perhaps something here will please you."

Cora turned back to Mrs. Proud, and immediately a pretty blue figured muslin claimed her eye. For a little while they discussed the gowns, but at last Cora felt she might query Mrs. Proud about the residents of Wintercroft. She was pleasantly surprised that Mrs. Proud, now comfortable with Cora and the prospect of a new customer, was quite willing to enjoy a chat about the town's wealthy neighbor without waiting for Cora to open the subject.

"Lord Wintercroft bought much of Mrs. Joanna's wedding clothes from me." Mrs. Proud brushed her fingers over a pretty yellow silk crepe lying on the table between them, smoothing out a wrinkle. "Mrs. Joanna had nothing, you know. All of her clothes came from Lord Wintercroft. He would do anything for his son."

"Mr. Arthur Neadow?"

"Yes. What a pity when he died." She drew a copy of *La Belle Assemblée* from the shelf behind her and opened it to a marked page. "Here is a very good style for you in a morning gown. It has two flounces at the hem and a nice full sleeve gathered at the cuff." She tapped the drawing with a finger. "Might you be marrying Mr. Alexander?"

Cora nearly choked and was forced to cough.

"I shall fetch you a glass of water!" exclaimed Mrs. Proud, jumping to her feet.

"No," Cora croaked.

"You do not want it?"

"No—I am *not* marrying—Mr. Alexander."

Mrs. Proud scurried into the back room and presently returned with the water.

"I thought that perhaps . . ." Mrs. Proud began, holding out the cup. "And I do not mean to pry . . . but as Lord Wintercroft is buying your clothes . . ."

"I am engaged to Lord Wintercroft." Cora took the cup and sipped.

Mrs. Proud stopped in midsentence. Her eyes went wide, she stuttered, and then she found her voice.

"Oh, my dear! I see. I congratulate you. I of course did not *really* suppose you were marrying Mr. Alexander. Lord Wintercroft would never be buying these gowns. It is known by everybody that Lord Wintercroft and his son . . . Well, perhaps I have said too much."

"Oh, no! Pray tell me all. I am to marry into the household, so I must know."

Mrs. Proud needed no further convincing.

"That is true, and quite right you are! Well, Mr. Alexander went away years ago. I should say it was right about the time Mr. Arthur married Mrs. Joanna."

Mrs. Proud seated herself once more and continued. "Mr. Alexander returned to pay his respects when Mr. Arthur died. He was barely here a day, then he went off and joined the army and never came back. Some say Lord Wintercroft drove him off, and some say it broke Lord Wintercroft's heart."

"How terribly sad."

"Why Mr. Alexander has returned now is anybody's guess, but some say he's worried for his inheritance."

"I see."

"Oh, dear! You mustn't believe I meant that is on

your account! It is all of the others up there. One by one they came to stay, and I imagine Mr. Alexander got wind of it."

Mrs. Proud's pale face actually gained color, and Cora, who was not at all offended, sought to reassure her. "I am sure no one is thinking of me *quite* yet. I have only just come. How did Mr. Arthur die?"

"You do not know?" Mrs. Proud's eyes widened. "Someone has been very remiss in not telling you, then. Mr. Arthur went walking alone along the cliffs. It was a horrible thing. He fell from Beachy Head."

Although Cora had not yet seen the cliffs, she knew of their height, particularly the famous height of the one named Beachy Head. A fall from there would mean instant death. It seemed that not only was Mr. Arthur's demise a tragedy but the circumstances were fraught with speculation.

"How dreadful."

Mrs. Proud leaned forward then, a conspiratorial glitter in her eyes. "Some say Mr. Alexander *murdered* Mr. Arthur. I do not believe *that*, mind you. It's just wagging tongues."

Good Lord. This was more than Cora had bargained for. Was it possible? And if so, why? Arthur was the younger brother after all, so there could have been no issue of inheritance.

"Mr. Alexander, of course, was not home at the time," Cora said.

Mrs. Proud waved a hand. "Some say this, some say that. But *I* say he would not have done it. Mr. Arthur was his brother, and blood is blood. Why would a man murder his brother with no reason?"

"I quite agree."

Mrs. Proud sighed. "Lord Wintercroft doted on Mr. Arthur. He gave him everything. Everyone liked Mr. Arthur. He was a cheery man and all, and open-handed in his ways. And handsome! All the young women were half in love with him. He liked to visit the Tiger when he was at home, and was just as comfortable as anything."

"And Mr. Alexander?"

"Oh, he was very different. He was rarely in town, and when he did come, he was very grave and went about his business. I heard it told he was a wild youth, mind you, and with quite the temper! I must say that one *wished* that Mr. Arthur was the older, but of course Mr. Alexander was. And then Mr. Arthur died. There were many sad faces in town that day."

Cora's mind was busy with what she had heard, and she was torn between chatting longer and finding Birdie. Mrs. Proud was in form to talk, and Cora was interested in hearing what she had to say. Then Cora noticed the time.

"I feel I am set now, and I must go and find Birdie. Do you know where she might have gone?"

"Birdie? To her mum's, to be sure. It is a bit of a walk from here. She is a good girl. So she is to be your personal maid? She is telling her mum all about it, she is. She will be back in a trice." Mrs. Proud lifted a little wooden box from the shelf behind her, and from it took a length of finely worked lace. "This would look lovely on the yellow silk. And did you know that Mr. Alexander was once married?"

As a delaying tactic, this worked very well. "No, I did not."

"He was," Mrs. Proud said. "It wasn't spoken of much—it was after he went away. The young woman died a few months after the wedding."

"Oh, dear."

"Some say he was affected by it in a bad way."

"Do you mean he is even more ill-tempered now than he used to be?"

Cora could have bitten her tongue, but she was reassured by Mrs. Proud's smile.

"At least you will not have it that he murdered her as well as his brother, as some say! It is quite a story at Wintercroft, isn't it? But a bride *does* need to know these things."

Cora concluded her business with Mrs. Proud at last and stepped out upon the street. The driver, Will, and the carriage could not be far. At least, she dearly hoped that was true, for her mind was too full of tumultuous thoughts of Alexander Neadow to go about looking for them.

But she was correct; the carriage was not far at all. It was in front of the Tiger.

Cora stood for a moment, gazing at the Tiger, considering her situation. Birdie was missing, but likely at her mother's, supposedly a good walk from here; Will was at the Tiger, likely becoming less able to drive the carriage by the minute; and she had agreed to marry a man whose one son had died in suspicious circumstances and whose other son had not only been accused of his brother's murder but had been widowed in circumstances that had yet been unexplained. One might add that the surviving son and father shared a common dislike of one another, that both were bad-tempered and self-absorbed, and that Cora's seamstress plied her trade with smuggled goods.

Yes, indeed, the nighttime trade is alive in East Dean. Cora knew about smuggling. In Yorkshire it was a very known thing, and she knew that the source of Mrs. Proud's exquisite silks had to be an illegal one. Mrs. Proud would not have been able to afford the duty on such fabrics.

There were other things that might come by boat in the dark of night, of course. It must be common knowledge.

Cora stared at the Tiger.

At last she sighed. She must not speculate about smuggling, or wonder if Wintercroft had any connection to it. That was quite an absurd idea, in fact. She was coming to expect ill news about the household at every turn. She had decided to accept the challenge of Wintercroft and set it to rights; she could not cower at every little obstacle.

So she added one more task to her list: that of discovering what had happened to Mr. Arthur. Then she squared her shoulders and set off at a smart pace for the Tiger.

Alex reined in his horse and gazed out over the ocean toward the blue horizon. He was looking toward France; Wintercroft was behind him, where all were accounted for save four—Miss Cora MacLaren,

Birdie the maid, Will the coachman, and Alex's cousin Roland.

If Miss MacLaren had gone alone to East Dean, Alex would have expected that she was about nothing more than the stated jaunt to the dressmaker's. The fact that Roland was gone as well made it a different matter.

Roland had expressed the intention of playing a game of billiards after tea, but when Alex had checked, only Bertram and Robert were in the billiards room. Alex was considerably annoyed that he had allowed Roland to slip away so easily.

Alex was working on the guess that Roland had gone to visit the Tiger, where he could quietly gather news about local activities. It could not be ruled out that he also meant to meet Miss MacLaren—and so Alex was riding to East Dean.

Unfortunately, Roland had the advantage of an earlier start.

Alex abandoned the ocean vista and turned his horse back onto the road south. He had no objection to watching Miss MacLaren today. He simply had too many people to watch. Bertram had gone on his usual afternoon stroll before the game of billiards, and Lord Wintercroft had retired to his study. Alex's aunt Eliza had settled in the drawing room with Robert's wife, Mirabelle—not that there was any reason to keep watch on such a simple woman as Robert's wife. Finally, there was Joanna. Joanna had gone to the nursery to read to Augie. She was, of course, above suspicion.

If Roland had remained at Wintercroft to play billiards with Robert and Bertram, Alex would have passed on following Miss MacLaren in favor of keeping watch at home. Even so, one did not dismiss the idea that she would be a foolish woman indeed to turn down any chance to better her situation—and she might stumble across the opportunity sooner than he might guess.

Well, there were *certain* offers she would decline, he supposed. Alex urged his horse into a canter, remembering Miss MacLaren's fit of temper in the garden after he had kissed her. She did appear to have standards of a sort, did his pretty foe, but all the same, he would not elevate her above the pecuniary ambitions of the rest of his family. She would be alert to other methods of filling her purse, since a woman as clever as he deemed Miss MacLaren to be would not count on his father to make her fortune.

The last thing he wanted was another smuggler in the family—especially married to his father.

And so Alex, who believed his entire family was either mad or corrupt, continued toward East Dean on the trail of his cousins Roland and Miss MacLaren.

Roland proved easy to find. Alex dismounted at the Tiger and, upon entering, spotted his cousin at a corner table lifting a mug with three companions. As was his habit, Alex hesitated in the doorway, scanning the rest of the room for any signs of danger in the dim interior. Besides Roland's group, there were several other locals in the place, all farmers or local tradesmen.

Roland, who had none of Alex's hesitation, called out his greeting.

"Halloo, cousin! What brings you here?"

Alex, satisfied that he might proceed, walked slowly across the room to Roland's table, where he stopped. The room had fallen silent. Alexander was not one of them; even when he had lived here, he had not been one of them. It was interesting that Roland was.

Roland lolled back on his chair, his neat tailored coat hanging open, one elbow on the table and the other hand engaged in holding his mug aloft. His white neckcloth was slightly loosened, but that was the only compromise in the elegance of his attire. He sat with his circle of confederates, whose common dress was in stark contrast to his tonnish fashion, but none of them seemed to notice.

Roland gave Alex a roguish smile. "How fine for you to join us, cousin! It is as good a way as any to pass a few trifling hours. I must say, however, you surprise me, welcome though you are. What might bring you here today?"

Alex lowered his lids slightly and held his gaze to Roland's puckish face. "When you did not appear for billiards, I had nothing better to do."

"I never knew you to play."

"It has been several years since you have known anything of me."

Roland chuckled. "True! True. You have the better of me there."

"And what of yourself? What brings you to town?"

One by one, Roland's companions had quietly slipped away. Alex drew out a chair and seated himself, facing Roland.

Roland lifted his brows. "Me? How can you ask?" He raised his mug and took a sip. "I, dear cousin, am but an impartial, unbiased observer. I enjoy watching life being lived in all of its manifestations. It might surprise you to know that the simple people of this village are much more interesting to observe than my boring assortment of relations. Yourself excepted, of course."

"Am I interesting to watch?"

Roland burst into a laugh. "You must excuse me! Dear Lord, but you are amusing! Of course you are interesting to watch! The very reason you descended upon us for a visit is interesting. Why, it is enough to entertain me for several days at least—then you must do something, or you will bore me like the rest."

Alex fought not to smile; it was very difficult. Roland was hard to resist, and was in fact his favorite of his relatives. Roland had a wicked sense of humor and a very dry wit, which was entertaining when he was not trying excessively hard to annoy.

Roland also preferred an expensive lifestyle, and Roland had no money—at least, none that was apparent. Roland could be at Wintercroft to rusticate until his next quarter day—or he could be about something else entirely. That was the reason Alex was watching him.

"You must be content, then," Alex responded, "as

I am doing something now. I hope you will find me very enlivening. Have you seen Miss MacLaren in town?"

"Ah, so that is it!" Roland's eyes took on an amused gleam. "The fair Miss MacLaren! Now I wonder if you are seeking amusement with her, or are you looking for an opportunity to rid us of her inconvenient presence?"

"And why should I do anyone such a favor? She is no inconvenience to *me*." Alex gave Roland a hard look. "Pray be cautious with your jokes, for some take them seriously."

"Dear me. How I forget. It has been how many years since poor Arthur took his misstep? Three? No, it is four. I have been ghastly rude! I am *so* sorry, old fellow!"

"You are not in the least, but I shall let that pass. So have you seen her?"

Roland grinned. "As a matter of fact, I have. The young lady strolled into the Tiger just as easy as you please and separated poor Will from his pint. They have gone somewhere or other."

Alex started in surprise. "She was alone?"

"Quite. She didn't seem a bit concerned. I offered my assistance, of course, but she declined."

"Where did she go?"

Roland shrugged. "All I know is that she asked for directions to a . . . let me think . . . a Mrs. Cooper's."

"Would she be the dressmaker?"

Roland laughed. "I may be accused of a number of things, but not of frequenting a dressmaker's! At least, not without a plumper pocket and an appreciative female companion. I am afraid I cannot help you."

"No . . . no, her name is Proud," Alex said to himself, frowning. "Yes. Proud. I should have paid attention!"

Roland raised his fine brows. "Is there some skullduggery afoot? Pray tell. You know that I crave amusement."

"Where is this Mrs. Cooper's home?"

"My dear Alex, I have not the foggiest idea. But you might ask the proprietor. He is the one our Miss MacLaren spoke with."

Alex lost no time in procuring the directions and heading his horse to Mrs. Cooper's. He found the whitewashed cottage in short order. He also found three small boys and the vicar in the yard.

Alex dismounted and approached the vicar, the Reverend Mr. Phillip Nye, who was standing near the door. It had been four years since he had last spoken with the vicar; and at the moment he was very sorry to see the reverend in Mrs. Cooper's dooryard. He was uncertain why he was sorry, but the meeting made him feel distinctly uncomfortable.

"I am looking for Miss MacLaren," Alex said.

The vicar nodded. "Hello, Mr. Alex. I am pleased to see you as well." He smiled. "Miss MacLaren is here. Do you wish to speak with her?"

Alex nodded and started to pass the reverend, but Phillip held out his arm.

"I am afraid you cannot go in."

"Whyever not?"

As if to answer, a sharp scream came from within the cottage.

"Good Lord," Alex said.

"Exactly." The reverend grinned. "Mrs. Cooper's married daughter is giving birth."

Chapter Eight

"*I*t has been a very long time since I saw you last," said Reverend Nye. "I remember you clearly at your brother's funeral, but I do not believe we exchanged three words."

"I must apologize, then. It was the occasion." Alex fidgeted and glanced toward the closed cottage door. It would not open any sooner, however. He was trapped with Reverend Nye.

"I understand. But then I heard you had gone away again."

Alex looked at his older acquaintance, trying to dismiss the ghastly images of childbirth, with Miss MacLaren in the midst of it, from his mind. At least, he suspected she was in the midst of it.

Phillip Nye was younger than Alex's father, straight as a reed and still handsome in spite of the gray in his auburn hair. Alex had known the reverend since his boyhood, and the reverend had been the only man to show him kindness as a child. Today, his concern could not be questioned.

Alex's discomfort was not the fault of the reverend. The fault was his own.

"One faces one's responsibilities eventually," Alex said.

"One hopes. But I wonder what you consider to be your responsibility? You are a military man, Alex. Some believe you are here to spy on the good folks of East Dean."

Alex held the reverend's gaze. It told him nothing. "My concern," Alex said levelly, "is for my father. That is all."

The reverend nodded. "As it should be. I realize it is not a pleasant duty for you, Alex, but you are a man today, not the boy I knew. You shall do the correct thing." He paused. "I met Miss MacLaren today," he said. "A very agreeable young woman. We had no time to converse, but I understand her father was a doctor. I hope everyone is well at Wintercroft?"

"Yes. Quite well."

"I am very happy to hear that. Then you have no bad news to tell Miss MacLaren?"

Damn. This was what he had forgotten about Reverend Nye. The blessed man could ferret a secret out of the devil himself.

"She is my cousin," Alex said, hoping their relationship would justify his presence.

"Hm. That is interesting, but I should not call it bad news. Not for you, at the least of it."

The twinkle in Reverend Nye's eyes was not lost on Alex. Neither was the inference.

"I am afraid you are mistaken." Alex looked back

at the cottage door and studied it intently. It seemed that his neckcloth was tightening, closing off his throat. Thank the Lord that the reverend did not know the whole of it.

"Am I? You are a widower, still in the prime of life. Within the cottage is a very interesting young lady who, very conveniently—I might say providentially—is your cousin. I assume that the connection is a distant one, knowing your family as I do, and since you have already made her acquaintance I conjecture she is staying at Wintercroft. No, I could not possibly be mistaken."

Alex let out a pent-up breath. There was no help for it now; the reverend would learn it in any case.

"She is engaged to marry my father."

For a moment there was nothing but dead silence from the reverend. As it dragged on, Alex forced himself to look at the man again.

He was frowning, and his eyes locked on Alex's. "I find that highly incredible."

"I should also, if I did not know it is true. My father announced it at table last night, and she did not deny it."

The reverend let out a sound of disgust. "The old foo— The sad old fellow. This is very lamentable. She is being compelled by circumstance."

For the first time a smile twitched at the corners of Alex's lips. "Your first assessment is correct. He is an old fool."

The conversation ended there. Alex was left with stirred emotions that he had long ago shut away—or so he had believed. He was anxious to see Miss

MacLaren and escape the reverend's haunting presence, but he had to be satisfied with waiting some minutes longer. He tried to distract himself by pondering Miss MacLaren's strange behavior.

He had to conclude that she was not, after all, consorting with smugglers—admittedly an unlikely possibility at the outset. She had had no prior contact with the area before her arrival, he was quite certain, and it was a bit much to believe her to be involved with the local intrigue within twenty-four hours. And certainly not at this moment.

He began to feel rather foolish.

An infant's cry erupted from within the cottage.

At last the door opened. Miss MacLaren stepped forth, wearing a soiled apron and a happy smile, her thick red hair askew. Her gaze quickly found the Cooper boys.

"It is a boy, and Becky is well! You boys will need to—" Miss MacLaren stopped speaking at the exact moment she spied Alex standing beside the reverend.

Alex nodded politely. "Miss MacLaren."

Her cheeks, already pink from exertion and excitement, seemed to grow even pinker. "Mr. Alexander. Whatever are you doing here?"

He had to admit to himself that she was perhaps the most alluring female of his acquaintance. There she stood, in her old brown gown and hideous apron, her red hair tumbling down and her face flushed like a harlot's fresh from a warm bed, her body taut with surprise and blooming with vitality and health. And then there were her clear green eyes, sharp, probing, and oh so shrewd.

"I was looking for you," he said evenly, "in the event you needed any assistance."

She blinked. "That is very odd. You wished to assist me at the dressmaker's?"

For the first time—he could swear it was the first time—in many years, he felt heat rising in his own face.

"No. I did not believe you needed my help there." He paused, and then could not resist adding, "Assuming, of course, your dress at dinner last night was not of your own choosing."

He was rewarded by seeing the fire leap back into her eyes.

"You, sir, seem to take pleasure in tormenting others. How very like your father you are."

How very like your father you are. The line struck Alex like the report of a musket. His first impulse of vehement denial was immediately arrested by a horrifying thought. *Am I like my father?*

Reverend Nye cleared his throat. "This is a time for happiness and celebration. Let us not visit discord upon the new mother and child."

Reverend Nye might be older and grayer now, but his kindness remained unchanged.

Alex felt ashamed. "You are correct. I am very sorry, Miss MacLaren."

She stared at him a moment, gazing at his face as if it were suddenly odd. At last she said, "Very well, then I am also. I appreciate your concern for me."

There was no time for him to judge the emotion in her eyes, her too careful tone of voice. At that moment the door opened again and little Birdie popped out.

"Becky has fed the baby, and now she is asleep. Mum says that you boys should go—" Her glance took in Miss MacLaren and the two gentlemen, and she froze with lips parted.

Alex recognized the little maid, and the pieces fell into place. Miss MacLaren had been helping Birdie's sister.

Miss MacLaren briskly interceded on Birdie's behalf. "Boys, you are to go to your uncle's now. You may come home at suppertime. Birdie, would you like to stay here for the night? I shall do very well by myself."

"But I have me duties in the kitchen. Cook will have me turned off!"

"I shall take care of that. You are to stay, Birdie."

"That is a very kind offer," said the reverend. "Birdie, tell your mother that I shall not need her for a few days. I shall stop over tomorrow to see the new mother." He turned to Miss MacLaren. "It has been a great pleasure to meet you. I hope we may visit again soon. Come along, boys—you may walk with me."

Miss MacLaren responded to the reverend with a warm smile and an equally friendly good-bye, and as the reverend and the boys walked away, Alex felt a surprising surge of jealousy. It might be natural for Miss MacLaren to bestow her smile in thanks for kindness, but Alex's emotion was not reasonable.

He wanted her to smile for *him*, in spite of it all—

and in spite of the necessity of keeping his distance. He had to keep his head clear. He could trust no one, including the intrepid Miss MacLaren.

Miss MacLaren urged Birdie back inside the cottage and then turned again to Alex. "If you would wait a moment."

He felt absurdly hopeful. "Of course."

She disappeared within the cottage, but came out in a few minutes, the apron gone and her bonnet fixed neatly over her hair.

"You may help me to find Will," she said. "He is walking the horses. I should not be surprised if he has walked them back to the Tiger."

Alex felt a smile touch his lips. Miss MacLaren might be wreaking havoc with his family, but he approved of her today. He could think of no other lady of his acquaintance, past or present, who would have entered a pub unescorted in pursuit of her driver or given assistance to a stranger in childbed. Then there was the little matter of her trusting *him* after repelling his unwelcome advance the night before.

"You may ride my horse, then, and I shall walk with you."

"Nonsense. I shall walk while you go to fetch Will."

No, she did not quite feel trust toward him. But that she did not and was unafraid made him admire her even more.

"Miss MacLaren, I think you have had enough exercise for the day." He turned to his horse, which was a few steps away munching on wisps of grass, and caught the trailing reins. "Mischief is a good mount."

"Mischief?"

Alex turned Mischief around, then looked at Miss MacLaren. "Come. No tricks, no wild rides, no liberties of any kind—you have my solemn vow. I am attempting to be helpful."

She decided, and, when she did so, stepped forward briskly. It seemed to be a way with her, he thought; when she made up her mind she acted straightaway and without hesitation.

Wordlessly she placed her foot in his hands and allowed him to boost her up. Alex quickly fixed the near stirrup to accommodate her, and when she was settled, he began leading Mischief toward the Tiger.

He puzzled a few moments on how to question Miss MacLaren in a tactful way about what she had done inside the cottage. At last he said, "Were you able to give assistance?"

He expected an indifferent answer. He was surprised to receive more.

"Yes. The mother was having difficulties. Happily, with luck and ingenuity I did not need my father's instruments. It was not hard to set it to rights."

"That is fortunate."

"It is more fortunate that I happened to arrive when there was a need. Apparently there is no local doctor, and the midwife was visiting in the country. Something should be done."

So Miss MacLaren had been instrumental in delivering her maid's sister's infant. He knew the true

Miss MacLaren to be a doctor's daughter, so this Miss MacLaren was no impostor.

He reminded himself that she had not been raised a young woman of privilege, and yet in many ways she seemed every bit the lady. Her speech was refined, for instance, even if her temper was much less civilized. Miss MacLaren did not mince words.

"How do you come about your skills?"

"I understand you investigated my past, Mr. Alexander. If you did so, then you know my father was a physician. He was a very good one, as well."

"I understand. But this does not explain your own ability. A young woman is not expected to learn her father's profession."

"I learned at his side. I am not a doctor, but I am quite practiced. That is why I chose to care for the ill."

"My father is not ill, Miss MacLaren."

She was silent.

"I am not attempting to goad you. I am simply curious."

"Mr. Alexander," she said with sudden sharpness, "I have managed for myself for the past four years. I nursed a young mother back to health and two dear old women in their last months. But one does not toss opportunity aside without examining it. There is work to be done at Wintercroft."

Alex looked up at her. She was staring determinedly ahead between his horse's ears.

"Miss MacLaren, there are also things that are best left alone. You will find far more grief at Wintercroft than gratification."

"I am not seeking to be gratified, Mr. Alexander."

"Then by what word do you call it? For you are not doing it without reward to yourself. No one does."

He heard her sharp intake of breath. "I can likewise question *you*. I understand you have not been home in years, and yet suddenly you have appeared. It is clear that affection does not explain the matter. What reward do *you* seek?"

He found that he had no answer, and he found that it made him angry. He had reason to be here. He, of all persons, had reason! How dare she ask him such a question?

But this time his temper was fully under control. He would not rise to her bait. He had dealt with his father for many years; he could handle Miss MacLaren.

"Miss MacLaren, it is not to be thought that you can understand Wintercroft in a few hours, let alone have a plan to set it to rights. You may be experienced in birthing and dying, but I am experienced with the rest of life, and I beg to contradict you."

Alex waxed vehement as he spoke, and began walking faster. As he was leading Mischief, Mischief increased his pace as well.

"I am older than you are, I have served my country in battle, and I have more knowledge of the minds of men than you have. There is a great deal I could say to you, but I will not, save that it is a mistake to rely on the false confidence of youth. The world is *not* as it seems to you. Remedies are *not* the simple things you believe them to be. You would serve much better to examine yourself—"

"Mr. Alex—"

"—and study your own naïveté. As to the consequences you yourself create—"

"Zander, *slow down*!"

Alex stopped and turned in surprise. He saw Miss MacLaren, face flushed, eyes glittering, clinging to his saddle with the determination of a lioness clutching her prey.

"Sir, your saddle is meant for riding astride, and it is *highly* unsuited to ladies. If you doubt me, you may try riding it sidesaddle and see for yourself!"

He stared at her foolishly, his heart pounding in his throat, realizing that he had done the thing that he had felt impossible to do again—lose control with Miss MacLaren. "I beg your pardon."

"I shall not ride so that you can abuse me. Let me down. I prefer to walk!"

"I am truly sorry. It shall not happen again."

"As to that, you gave your word once. It shall not suffice a second time." Miss MacLaren began to disengage her foot from the stirrup.

"No." Alex stepped to her side and placed his hand over hers, stilling it on the leather strap.

Cora looked down at his hand, feeling its gentle strength through her glove, and snapped her gaze to his face. For a moment all she could do was stare—and it seemed it was all he could do as well, for his eyes never left hers.

His characteristically harsh face was changed. In the depths of his dark eyes she saw the pain of unmitigated sorrow—for the second time that afternoon.

His fingers curved around hers, gently lifting her hand from the stirrup strap.

"Please," he said quietly. "I may deserve to be shamed, but do not dismount. Just this time I ask your indulgence."

He was pleading with her. This angry Zander, this rude gentleman of dark secrets, was afraid to be humiliated before the townspeople. She blinked and felt dampness on her eyelids. He was still holding her hand, and she felt his warmth all the way to her heart.

She tilted her head back. "Very well." With a pang of regret she tugged her hand from his grasp. "But you must not treat me to any more such boorish behavior!"

"I shall not," he said. Then he smiled.

I must not lose my head. He believes me to be an enemy. I may be a softhearted fool if I like, but I must mind business. And I must on no account lose control of my temper again.

Cora rode home in the landaulet opposite the snoozing Will. Alex drove, and not without a protest from her; she had suggested herself for the duty, as she was used to driving her father's gig, and proposed that Mr. Alex ride his Mischief home. But Alex would have none of that, saying there was a world of difference between a landaulet and a one-horse gig, so Mischief trotted calmly behind the landaulet, his reins tethered to the rear of the carriage, while Alex drove. There was consequently no conversation, but Cora had time to consider the revelations of the day.

She had caught Mr. Alex out. She had read a clue in his eyes when she had accused him of being like his father—she had seldom seen such consternation. Second, when she had tried to leave him in town, she had glimpsed an immense grief in his eyes. Mr. Alex, first son and least loved, was masking a great hurt behind his brusque manner. He was not the heartless reprobate he made himself out to be.

He did not like her, of course. She was a threat to them all, and to him particularly, if one considered that Lord Wintercroft might still soften toward his only living son if it were not for the influence of a young bride. And she surely must not forget the mysterious death of Alex's brother, Arthur, no matter that she felt he was innocent.

Even without a financial motive, a man with an ungovernable temper could kill his brother in a fit of rage. She simply did not believe he had the heart to do such a thing.

It was unfortunate she could not tell them the truth, for she had no intention of marrying the tyrannical old codger, but she could not heal the discord at Wintercroft unless they all believed she would.

Cora sighed and closed her eyes, feeling the cool sea air wash over her face and the various jolts and bumps of the carriage. She was almost sick of this. She went from place to place and did her best, but she always moved on. It would become very hard as she grew old. What would become of her? But then . . . but then, her father had never questioned his calling, his fate. He had served with unquestioning loyalty until his end, leaving his eighteen-year-old daughter to fend for herself. He had prepared her to do just that.

But was this the life he had expected her to lead? Had he envisioned for her a life alone, a life without children or the companionship of a husband, helpmeet, and friend?

No, I chose this life. I chose it because I may do what I know best and do the most good. I am not a Mary Cooper giving birth while my husband is at sea, or a Mrs. Arthur Neadow trapped by marriage and early widowhood in the home of her bitter father-in-law. I am not a helpless Mrs. Robert Neadow, content to be managed by her husband. I am Cora MacLaren, a—a "wild Scotswoman."

Cora smiled to herself. If her feelings were bittersweet, at least she had reaffirmed her resolve. She would do her duty here, then find a life elsewhere.

Chapter Nine

*W*hen Cora returned to Wintercroft she went
looking for Cook. No one was apparent on
her arrival; there was not even the thought-
provoking distraction of Mr. Alex, as he had left her
in order to deposit Will and the horses at the stable.
Cora decided against seeking someone in the drawing room for directions, for since she was a persona
non grata she would possibly gain nothing but delay.
She would trust her now rested wits to find her way.

The kitchen was surely in its own wing. Recalling
that one wing of the house ran southeasterly toward
the sea from the old part of Wintercroft, Cora made
her way in this direction. She presently arrived at the
old hall where the widow Joanna Neadow had first
greeted her. Of the four doors in the cavernous room,
she had just entered by one, and one led to the courtyard. She would try one of the other two.

The first opened to a Romanesque portico that led
to parts unknown, perhaps to the stable. In any case,
it would not go to the kitchen, which she knew to

be below stairs. Cora closed this door and walked to the other. It opened on well-oiled hinges.

Aha! It was a dank passage with stairs leading downward, lit by distantly spaced candles. The smells of damp and of burning tallow wafted up the stairs to meet her as she descended. *This* must lead to the kitchen!

The amount of light in the passage left something to be desired. Along her way she noted two candles whose flames had extinguished entirely and several that were guttering badly. Since she expected she was in the company of rats, she resolved to improve the light here as soon as was practical. With this thought she continued fearlessly until she reached the door at the end of the passage.

The door was a heavy affair at the top of two shallow steps. Cora opened it without announcement and stepped into the kitchen. Before her was an open area, with a great fireplace at the opposite end. The central worktable, as well as the tables and shelves that lined the surrounding walls, was cluttered and dirty. A mound of dough lay abandoned on the table, a feast for flies, with a pot of cream beside it. Not a soul was to be seen.

Cora stared about her in mixed disgust and indignation. She reminded herself that the cook might not be to blame for the mess, and then set out to find her.

It did not take long. Cora stepped through a door into the scullery, then through another door into the brewery, and discovered a slatternly-looking woman sitting on a stool beside a barrel of brew, engaged in sampling it.

"Are you the cook?" Cora said crisply.

The woman looked up with bleary eyes. A few strings of gray hair escaped from beneath her cap, her apron was soiled beyond redemption, her stockings puddled around her ankles, and both of her shoes were run down at the heel and held together with strips of cloth.

For a long moment the woman did not answer, time enough for Cora to absorb the deplorable condition the woman was in. Even if sober, the cook would be a pitiful sight.

"Yes, mum, I am . . . the cook. And who . . . are you?"

"I am Miss Cora MacLaren."

The cook hiccupped. "Glory be," she said, and carefully lifted the dipper she held to her lips.

Cora was not in the least put off by this brazen display. "I demand your attention," she said. "And you are to stop drinking immediately." Cora held out her hand for the dipper.

The cook stared at her, and then she tossed the remainder of the beer on Cora's skirt.

"I'm done," she said. Then she grinned, showing a mouth of very bad teeth.

Cora had nursed many a stubborn patient and was determined not to lose her composure with a drunken cook. She took the dipper from the cook's hand and frowned at her. "That was not wise. I shall forgive you this once, for clearly you do not know what you are about. What is your name?"

The cook blinked owlishly. "I am Mrs. Potts," she

said with considerable dignity. "This is *my* kitchen, and I ain't never seen you before in my life. I—"

"No, you have not."

"—going to tell 'is lordship, is what I'll do."

"I happen to be the future mistress of Wintercroft, Mrs. Potts, and I shall be improving things here."

Mrs. Potts started to say something else, then stopped and stared at Cora blankly, as if understanding had at last penetrated her foggy brain.

"I will have this kitchen cleaned," Cora said. "And I will have *you* washed as well, unless you have the goodness to do it first. I will need a full inventory of what you have here, a list of your help, and a list of all they are responsible for. I will hire more if necessary, and I will let go anyone I must." Cora paused. "I hope that helps to explain who I am."

Mrs. Potts' blank face slowly changed. Before Cora's eyes, it transformed from anger to fear to grief. And then Mrs. Potts was sobbing into her filthy apron.

Oh, dear.

"Mrs. Potts, I did not say I am going to dismiss you."

". . . Can't do nothing . . . no help . . . I could die down here . . ."

"Mrs. Potts, I mean to help with the running of this kitchen. When I am done it will be a place to be proud of. Please stop weeping!"

It was some moments before Mrs. Potts calmed herself. Cora fumbled around the mess of a kitchen and found the used tea leaves drying on the counter.

There was enough water in the kettle to make Mrs. Potts a cup of weak tea.

Once the cook was settled in the chair in her little room off the kitchen with the tea and a sympathetic listener, she could not apologize enough for her behavior. After Cora had convinced her that she was quite forgiven, Mrs. Potts was ready to explain what was wrong with the kitchen.

"'Is lordship, he always was tight. But when young Arthur died, well, he just got so clutch-fisted there was nothin' left t' squeeze. He sent away most of th' help. It was terrible."

"Please go on."

"It was hard on th' families. There ain't a lot of positions hereabouts. I was left, because I'm the cook, and me brother was left because he drives the carriage. I still had one girl with me, but she worked for Mrs. Flynn, too—"

"Mrs. Flynn is the housekeeper?"

"Yes. And then he—'is lordship, that is—gets this bee in his bonnet to invite all his family t' live here. We had 'is lordship and Mr. Arthur's widow, 'is lordship's sister and her son. Then along comes Mr. Roland, and Mr. Robert and his wife, and then Mr. Alex comes home, and then—"

"And then I came."

Mrs. Potts sighed. "Yes, and then you came. I beg your pardon, mum, but 'is lordship wanted my Birdie to go and maid you, and so I get even less of the girl. You see how it goes. I just have to have help."

Cora took a settling breath. "Mrs. Potts, Birdie's

sister had her baby today. Birdie had to stay in town."

Mrs. Potts stared at Cora as if she had grown a third eye. "And who let her do that?"

It was clear that Mrs. Potts was unable to manage unless Cora found another maidservant—or helped Mrs. Potts with the evening meal herself.

"I did. So I will have to do something about it."

A more sober Mrs. Potts returned to the worktable and the neglected bread dough. Cora silently joined her to begin clearing the table of dirtied pots and clutter. Mrs. Potts kept working at the bread without looking up, and several minutes passed in this manner.

At last Mrs. Potts spoke. "If you don't mind me saying so, mum, you shouldn't be doin' that work."

"Someone must, and it appears there is no one but me." Cora picked up a stack of dirty pots and turned toward the scullery.

"You needn't. You can get Mrs. Mason in the village."

Cora turned to look back at her, balancing the stack of tinware against her chest. "Mrs. Mason?"

"She is my cousin. Used to work here with me, until 'is lordship turned her off." Mrs. Potts sniffed contemptuously. "She'd come."

Cora took a breath of relief. "Then you shall have her back," she said.

Mrs. Potts grunted. "Maybe. We'll see how long you stay."

Cora strode into the drawing room and came to a dead stop in the center. It effectively gained everyone's attention, as she was positioned where she could not be missed. Eliza Plymtree and Mirabelle Neadow looked up from their needlework, Eliza's son, Bertram, gazed at her from the side table, where he was building a house of cards, and Joanna Neadow glanced up from a corner chair, where she was reading a book.

Cora raised her chin and affected her most confident air. "I am in need of assistance." She looked from face to face, reading the various expressions of surprise and annoyance. Bertram, the only gentleman present, rose to his feet. She turned to him.

"I need someone to go to East Dean and fetch a Mrs. Mason. She is needed in the kitchen."

Bertram blinked. "I suppose—that is, I would be happy to—"

"Bertram, you shall do no such thing!" His mother rested her embroidery in her lap and glared at Cora. "You are not to listen to *her*. Go and fetch your uncle."

"Yes, Mother."

Cora fixed Bertram with a compelling look. "I should not, Mr. Bertram, if I wished to have my dinner tonight."

"Bertram! Go to your uncle this minute!" snapped Eliza.

Wordlessly, Joanna stood and left the room.

Cora sighed and turned to Eliza. "Mrs. Plymtree—"

"Now see what you have done!" Eliza said. "It is Joanna's duty to handle such matters! How dare you insult her again?"

"I did not mean to." Cora walked hesitantly up to Eliza and stopped before her. "Mrs. Plymtree, I need advice. Perhaps I might turn to you."

Eliza was now fixed on her needlework again, a scowl on her face.

"Mrs. Potts is alone in the kitchen," Cora said quietly. "She cannot prepare dinner and serve it without help. I am sure Lord Wintercroft will be upset if his dinner is ruined."

For another moment Eliza was silent. Then she looked up. "Bertram, go and fetch Mrs. Mason, and waste no time about it!"

"Yes, Mother."

Bertram left the room, Eliza went back to her needlework, and Cora breathed deeply in relief.

"Thank you, Mrs. Plymtree."

Cora took herself off without further ado, wondering if indeed she would be sent away on the morrow. Her life was very much like Bertram's house of cards; one misstep and all would come tumbling down. Somehow she must win over her enemies, one by one—even the mysterious Joanna. As for Mr. Alex . . .

A small bubble of pain grew in her breast. There was no possibility of winning over Mr. Alex. He was the spurned son and he hated her for taking all from him. If only it was possible to tell him otherwise.

It seemed best to get the worst done with first, so Cora tidied herself and went to find Lord Wintercroft. He was in his library, and he received her pleasantly enough.

Cora immediately informed him that it was necessary to hire someone for the kitchen work, and to her surprise, he offered no objection. Encouraged, she told him of the need for an additional maid or two, given the number living at Wintercroft. This time he frowned, but then, as if remembering himself, he again acquiesced. Then he asked her about her foray to the dressmaker's and offered his opinion that she had not ordered nearly enough.

Cora informed him that she would buy what she needed and no more. He said they would see, and the interview ended on a friendly note.

Cora left feeling considerably relieved, and decided to find Joanna. Joanna was a mystery, appearing as more of a shadow than a person, although a startlingly beautiful shadow. Joanna said little and evoked a sense of undying sorrow—and, as Cora had perceived, resentment of Cora herself. There was no wonder in that, however. Lord Wintercroft's pronouncement about redirecting his fortune had pleased no one but him.

Joanna was in the garden, seated beside the fountain and watching little Augie chase a butterfly with his net. Cora was reluctant to disturb this domestic scene, but she knew she must.

Joanna did not see her approach, so as she neared, Cora softly called out her name. Joanna turned her head, and a look of surprise quickly turned to an expressionless blank.

"I have been looking for an opportunity to speak with you," Cora said.

Joanna nodded, indicating that she might sit beside

her. Cora did so and then gazed at Joanna's beautiful profile, for Joanna was again watching her son.

"I do not want you to think badly of me," Cora said. "If I have made mistakes, I beg your forgiveness. I did not know it was your gown I wore last night, and I did not mean to intrude on your duties today."

Joanna replied without looking at her. "I know."

"Do you? I do not understand. I can see no means by which you could know why I have done as I have."

"I know my father-in-law. That is why I know." She paused, and Cora did not think she would say more, but she continued. "He meant to discomfit me when he borrowed my gown for you. Of course, he did not know it means nothing to me. I shall never wear those clothes again."

Cora fumbled for a rational reply. "Of course you would not. You would need gowns in the newer fashion."

"That is not the reason. I care nothing for fashion. I care nothing for any of this. I care only for my son."

Joanna had placed a subtle emphasis on the word "son." She clutched her black-mitted hands together in her lap, and they fretted nervously as she gazed at her only child. It was an unconscious display of emotion, for nothing else about her moved except for a strand of black hair in the breeze.

"Your son is a beautiful child. You must be proud." Cora paused, but Joanna did not answer.

"I learned of a situation in the kitchen today,"

Cora continued, "and acted on it, not knowing what else to do. I know that Lord Wintercroft is . . . frugal with his household spending, so I did not go to him. I had no idea that I might be offending you."

"You did not. You did me a service. I should have let him go without a supper. He would still blame me, but he would have been angrier if I had ventured to mend the problem first."

"I see. I suppose that is very wise. In any case, there will be another maid or two very soon."

"I should make clear that I do not stay here because I wish to," Joanna said then. "Lord Wintercroft promised to favor my son if I remained. Neither would he support me if I left. And so I have stayed on the force of his promise."

Cora could not think of a way to reassure Joanna that her son's inheritance was not at risk on Cora's account. That, she felt, was something Joanna would have to learn in time—but a response was required.

"I am not seeking Lord Wintercroft's fortune."

Joanna raised her elegant chin. "Miss MacLaren, that is an easy thing to say when you have his assurance that you will receive it. But I am pointing out to you that Lord Wintercroft's promises cannot be counted upon. He is prone to changing his plans."

"That I do not doubt. I count upon nothing. My life has taught me that lesson."

Joanna was silent for a moment. Cora sat with her, gazing over the garden and watching the small boy bobbing through the shrubbery in quest of an interesting bug.

"I saw you last night with Alex," Joanna said suddenly.

Cora stared at her in surprise. "I had been lost in the maze, and he led me out."

"You need explain nothing to me. It is for your benefit that I say this. It is wrong to love one man and marry another, expecting that you will not pay a price. You shall. In my case and in yours, not even death can make it right. I cannot marry my brother-in-law, and you cannot marry your son-in-law. I suggest you not be hasty."

"I assure you I am not interested in Mr. Alex!"

"Your words to me mean nothing. What you understand in your heart means all."

Joanna arose and called to her son.

"But I want to catch him, Mother!" Augie cried, pointing at the large blue butterfly fluttering over the honeysuckle. Still, the boy came running up to Joanna, trailing his net, and she caught his little hand.

"It is time to go in," she said. And before Cora could think of another thing to say, Joanna and her son were walking toward the terrace steps.

It took Cora a little while to understand what particularly bothered her about what Joanna had told her.

After Cora had left the maze with Alex, they had done nothing more than come indoors. Joanna could not have witnessed anything of a more intimate nature unless she had been inside the maze.

Chapter Ten

Cora's conversation with Joanna had a disturbing effect on her. Cora could not grasp why Joanna believed she had an interest in Mr. Alexander Neadow, particularly if she had been a witness to the incident in the maze. Yet, even as she thought this, she felt an emotion stir within for Alex that was not dislike.

It was concern, she thought. The small glimpse she had had into his soul today had given her a sympathy for him. It was nothing more than that, for he was capable of being so horridly contemptible when he chose that she could not possibly feel *affection* for him.

On the other hand, could she not understand why he might be inclined to mortify her? It was not the ordinary thing for an unknown young woman to supersede the eldest son in both place and fortune. Mr. Alex would have the title, but that was all.

Yet, if she understood matters correctly, Mr. Alex and his father were in such a state of umbrage with each other that her arrival at Wintercroft likely had little to do with the present state of affairs.

Cora went to bed no more enlightened about Mr. Alex. She had not seen him since the afternoon, as he, as well as Joanna and Mr. Roland, had been missing from the dinner table. Those remaining, including Lord Wintercroft, were disinclined to speak.

The puzzle kept her awake into the night. In the light of a new day Cora resolved to stop thinking about Mr. Alex and go about her mission of recovering Wintercroft from the brink of devastation.

She arose in blessed privacy and completed her toilet with cold water left from the evening before, dressed herself, and descended to the breakfast room at an early hour. Some slices of toast and the remains of a platter of cold ham lay on the buffet, along with a pot of tepid tea.

Whoever had risen before her was gone now, so Cora made short work of a meal and sought Lord Wintercroft to inform him of her plans for the day. She found only his sleepy manservant, who informed her that he had already gone out, so she asked him to convey that she was off to East Dean that morning to see about her gowns.

That was only partly the truth. She meant to check on Becky and to convey Birdie home to Wintercroft. She also intended to visit the vicar. In her brief meeting with him she had sensed he was a man of good understanding and a generous heart, and she suspected there was much he could tell her about Wintercroft and about Alexander Neadow.

Her plan was not so easily accomplished. She

learned that Will was gone, having been summoned to drive his master. Not deterred, Cora made her way to the stable in hopes of discovering another means of transportation.

She stepped into the cool interior of the old stone structure and was immediately enveloped in the scent of straw and horse. She stood a moment to allow her eyes to adjust to the dim light, and was happily surprised to find the stable was well kept. She needed to explore only a moment more to discover a boy cleaning one of the boxes.

"Boy, is there some conveyance I may use?"

He looked up, surprise clear on his face. "Mum?"

"I wish to go to East Dean."

He blinked. "Th' cart, mum. But ye must be able t' drive it."

"Then please put a horse to it."

And so it happened that Cora found herself on the road, driving the very cart that had brought her to Wintercroft. The cart was, after all, not so very different from the gig her father had let her drive, and she felt a welcome rush of lost freedom as she set old Caesar to a shambling trot and felt the wind of adventure in her face.

She reached East Dean much faster than she remembered from her first trip. She immediately drove to Mrs. Cooper's cottage, where she found Becky up in a chair nursing her new baby.

Becky smiled shyly at her when she entered, and Mrs. Cooper greeted her warmly.

" 'Tis you! You are an angel, that's what you are. The reverend says you were heaven-sent. I hate to think what would have happened if I'd had to birth Becky by meself!"

Mrs. Cooper was a sturdily built woman with a lined face, her person a testimony to a life of hardship, but she had a smile that told all about her ability to survive. It was simple indeed to smile back at her.

"I should have been devastated if I had not been here to help. Becky, how are you?"

Becky was indeed doing remarkably well. Cora found no reason for concern, and she noted that the little cottage was swept clean, the linens were fresh, and there was a pot of stew on the fire.

Birdie was not there, however. Mrs. Cooper explained that she had walked to the farm with her younger brother and would return with a jug of milk.

"Do you know that Mr. Alexander came by?" she added. "He did, just a very short while ago, with the most beautiful cut of mutton. I was never so thunderstruck!"

Cora, who was something like thunderstruck herself, acknowledged the goodness of the gift, and left the cottage with an even more confused image of Alexander Neadow.

Her next stop was Mrs. Proud's establishment, where she approved the work that had been done on the first gown and stood for some measurements, while listening to more gossip with little information of importance. Mrs. Proud did mention hearing of Mrs. Mason's being called back to Wintercroft and hoped that this meant that other employment was to follow.

Cora reassured her that it would, and quickly received the recommendation of Mrs. Proud's niece and nephew. Cora told her that they might apply in person, and sometime later she was able to escape and continue on to her third stop of the morning.

She found Reverend Nye in his garden behind the rectory. In a small square of land he had a patch of a kitchen garden and a beautifully wild profusion of country flowers—candytuft, lady's-smock, lavender, lupines, sweet Williams and poppies, Canterbury bells, larkspur, and hollyhocks. The reverend made an interesting picture in his gardening smock, into which he was gathering stems for a bouquet. He looked up and saw her, and straightened with a smile.

"Miss MacLaren! Welcome. I had not expected to see you so soon."

"But I have so little to occupy myself that you should not be surprised at all."

"I cannot believe it. My understanding of you from our meeting yesterday is that you are a young woman of industry—and of considerable compassion."

He approached her and stopped before her, his smile gentling into a look of kind regard.

Cora felt a stab of shame. She had resolved not to tell anyone of her plans, but if the reverend were to know she was engaged to marry Lord Wintercroft, she hated for him not to know the truth of it.

"You must have heard the gossip about me."

"Gossip?" He assumed a quizzical expression and scratched his head.

"Has no one told you that I am to marry Lord Wintercroft?"

The reverend looked dumbfounded, and his hand fell to his side. "Is this true?"

"Yes. At least . . ."

"Go on."

"It is true," Cora said lamely.

"Come. Let us talk about this." The reverend gave her his arm, and they walked to a wooden bench that rested beneath a bower of honeysuckle.

"Is this truly what you want?" he asked.

That simple question, spoken with gentle concern, caught Cora unprepared. For one moment she feared she would dissolve into an emotional display for a reason she did not understand, but she was able to subdue the threat of tears and smile at him.

The reverend, she suddenly realized, was handsome as well as kind. His eyes were a pale blue flecked with gray; his face, although showing his maturity, was yet an attractive one. As she gazed at him, she thought of how much she missed her father.

"It was not my intent to become engaged to anyone," she said. "It was Lord Wintercroft's idea—and I fear it is a selfish one on his part. It is not a happy plan for his family."

"Of which you are one," Reverend Nye pointed out. "But you have consented?"

"Yes." She paused. "Wintercroft is in dire need of improvement, and the family needs my help. I needed to consent in order to stay."

He frowned slightly. "And when is the wedding to be?"

"There is no date set as yet."

"I wonder how you expect to help the family?"

Somehow Reverend Nye caused Cora to tell a deal more than she intended. At the end he fastened her with a perceptive look and said, "It is an admirable thing to be of help to those in need, but you must take care that your exercise is not one of pride. Shall you truly help your cousins, or shall you merely feel important in trying? I can tell you that I have known the Neadow family as long as I have been alive, and there has not been peace at Wintercroft for many years. I might add that people seldom change unless they will it themselves."

Cora, feeling the heat stealing into her face, took a steadying breath. "I thank you for your advice, Reverend Nye."

"You are thanking me," he said, smiling, "but you are really wishing me to the devil. I do not mind, however. I only wish to plant a seed in your mind."

"People seldom change unless they will it," she shot back, raising her brows archly.

He laughed. "Ah! But you see, I am endowed with a special ability that normal mortals lack. I am determined to change *you*."

She smiled back at him. "If that is the case, I wish you good luck, Reverend."

"I gather I need it!" He chuckled again. "But then, my flock does tend to be troublesome, so I am quite used to a challenge!"

"What a way to speak of us! As if we are all so

difficult! But that does put me in mind of a question."

His expression sobered. "What is it?"

"The townsfolk . . ." She hesitated, and then decided to be forthright. "There is smuggling here, Reverend. I have seen evidence of it, and I am worried that someone I know may be involved."

For a moment his somber eyes searched hers. Then he said, "And have you any knowledge of who that person may be?"

She sighed. "No. But the possibility is there."

"Then I shall advise you. Do not look to discover this person. Do not try to know about this subject at all. It is an old way of survival, Miss MacLaren, and it will be defended." He paused. "It is unsafe ground upon which to walk."

Cora felt the seriousness of his warning, and it sent a small chill of fear down her spine. Still, she knew she would make her own choices about the matter.

"I understand." She stood and brushed a clinging leaf from her skirt. "I am afraid it is time for me to go."

"How unfortunate!" he said, his voice sprightly once more. He stood also, smiling down at her. "And we have only begun to chat. If I may have your ear for one moment longer, I mean to ask you a special favor."

This instantly piqued her curiosity. "And what would that be?"

He leaned closer as if confiding a secret. "I request your indulgence for someone who is in need of a friend."

He gazed into her eyes and Cora waited breathlessly. Who might he mean? In a second she was certain of his answer. He would say, of course, Joanna.

"Alexander," he said quietly.

She stared at him.

He straightened. "Do not look so astonished! You would not feel so if you knew him as I do. I am not blind, my dear—I saw the way he provoked you yesterday. But believe me, his hard manner hides a great deal."

She realized that she was gaping and closed her mouth.

"Thank you for sharing your time with me," he said. "I have enjoyed it very much."

She licked her dry lips. "I am sorry. I must seem very rude."

"Not at all."

"I cannot believe all you have said. In all honesty, I must tell you so. But I promise to think about it."

"Very well. And promise me one thing more. If you are ever in need of assistance, come to me. My door is always open."

"Thank you."

"I am very sincere about my offer," he said as he walked her to her cart. "May I assist you in any way now?"

"Oh, no. I shall drive back to Mrs. Cooper's now and hopefully find Birdie at home, and then I shall drive us back to Wintercroft. I am quite set."

"My dear, I am going to visit Mrs. Cooper and the

new mother now myself. Suppose you allow me to drive Birdie home? I should enjoy the outing."

The reverend was persuasive and Cora was inclined to be persuaded, so in the end she agreed. Very soon she was on her way home to Wintercroft, alone with her thoughts and the sound of Caesar's hooves on the road toward the sea.

He saw her there. It surprised him, for she was alone. She had driven her cart off the road and walked some distance to the cliff's edge, leaving old Caesar grazing in the field behind her.

Alex drew his mount to a slow walk and gazed at the distant female figure silhouetted against the sky. It was as if she were at land's end—and for certain, she was that. There was nothing beyond her but a sheer chalk cliff and the sea.

He knew it was Cora, for it would not be Joanna, and no village nor farm woman would do anything so foolish as this. They had not the time or the interest in a walk to the sea for no other reason than to stare at it.

It was then he caught a flicker of movement from the corner of his eye. There, quite some distance from her but approaching her steadily was the figure of a man on foot. He came from the direction of Wintercroft.

Alex stared, uttered an oath, and abruptly set Mischief on a course across the field. Cora needed to know that she, in particular, should not make herself so vulnerable. He could not make up his mind whether she had no fear or whether she was that stupid!

There was little cover on the sweep of land leading up to the edge of the cliff, so one could easily see the approach of another. However, one did not *hear* it. Unless Cora turned by chance she would not know of the approach of either the walker or Alex. Of course, it being the light of day, Alex's presence alone would protect her. But before he had ridden down this road, there had been no one to bear witness.

He dismounted a little way from the edge of the cliff and set Mischief free to graze, as the ground tended to be soft and it would not do for Alex to save Miss MacLaren only to have Mischief's weight plummet them all into the sea. The cliff had a tendency to give way, sometimes by small bits but sometimes with a massive break that sent a great fall of chalk into the sea and onto the narrow strip of beach below.

Miss MacLaren was standing very close to the edge—so close it astonished him. The wind had blown her hat back so that it bobbed about behind her, attached to her by its ribbons, and her red hair was itself in the process of pulling free from its pins and whipping about her head like the snakes of Medusa.

Her cape and dress billowed out behind her as well. She seemed the veritable figurehead of a ship at sea except in living motion, staring ever forward.

What on earth was Miss MacLaren thinking?

Alex reached her at last. He was seized by the

impulse to grab her flapping cape and yank her to
safety, but he thought better of it and carefully circled the hurricane of her flying clothing to reach her
side. Then he firmly closed his hand around her
upper arm.

Miss MacLaren jolted and turned on him with hor-
ror in her eyes. Seeing him, her mouth dropped
open—and she fought back like a lioness.

He was stunned. He had expected she would be
relieved that it was he! Terrified for the both of them
and with her fighting for her life against him, he
dragged her away from the edge.

"Miss MacLaren! Miss Mac—" Here he was inter-
rupted by her flying hand and uttered a curse that
he generally saved for male company. He grabbed
her wrist.

"I am *saving* you! Damn—stop *assaulting* me!"

She landed a kick squarely on his shin. Unfortunately she was wearing hard-soled footwear, and he
gasped in pain, but he did not release her. And then
she suddenly stopped.

"What are you doing?" she shouted at him over
the wind. "Are you mad?"

"Yes!" he shouted back. "Unquestionably! Now let
us walk away from the edge!"

Suddenly cooperative, she walked with him
toward her cart. In truth she walked while he limped,
for the sting had not yet left his shin.

"I am sorry," she said when it was easier to hear,
"but I thought you were trying to throw me over."

He bit back a tempting retort. "No, Miss Mac-
Laren, I was saving you from yourself."

"I cannot see how."

"Precisely."

"Stop being obtuse. Say what you are thinking, or say nothing."

"Miss MacLaren, I saw a man approaching you and I dared not let you be."

"What man?" She looked about, and of course there was no one else within sight.

He sighed heavily. "There *was* a man. He was approaching on foot from the north. He is naturally gone now. He probably thinks I am doing his business for him."

"You had better explain what you mean."

"I think I am being quite clear. You are in danger of being introduced to the sea in a violent manner. You have not made friends here, Miss MacLaren."

She was silent a moment, walking at his side. When he glanced at her, she was watching the path of her feet through the sea grass.

"You are saying that someone would like to murder me."

"I am saying that you must be aware that this is a possibility. Your death would mean a fortune to someone else."

"Not you?"

He inhaled sharply and stared ahead at the cart as they approached it. "My father will do as he likes, and my father is in control of the cards and makes the rules of the game. No one knows whom he will favor in the end. It may or may not be you, Miss MacLaren. He himself may not know who it will be, or if he does, he enjoys keeping us guessing."

He paused and then added, "As for myself, I tired of his game long ago and count myself out of the play. I do not care one way or the other what he does."

They reached the cart. There was nothing left to do but help her to step into it and wait while she gathered the reins. When this was done, she gazed down at him. Her green-gold eyes were luminous and very steady.

"I thank you for your concern, however unnecessary," she said coolly. Then she switched Caesar and set off toward the road, leaving Alex to wonder if he was worried, angry, or out of his mind.

Chapter Eleven

*A*lex went about his business each day with a discipline honed by years in the military. He arose early, and as he completed his ablutions, he thought about what he had learned or observed on the previous day and what, if any, plans he had made as a result. He dressed with care to satisfy his father's censorious eyes, and then he consumed a very brief breakfast and set about the course he had decided upon.

This morning Alex reviewed all during his careful shave, which he performed without benefit of valet.

He had not yet found any material evidence that a smuggling operation was organized from his father's house, but he had not discovered information to the contrary, either. He had tried to link certain news to Roland's visits to East Dean, but so far he had not succeeded in that.

Robert seemed too staid to involve himself in anything so distastefully vulgar and illegal, but he appeared to be strapped financially, and his extended visit lent credence to this idea. No one with independent means would linger overlong in Lord Wintercroft's company, after all, and certainly not when one had a wife who was expecting—for if Alex did not miss his guess, the pretty and vacuous Mrs. Mirabelle Neadow was in the family way. And if this were the case, might that not drive Robert to consider a means of alleviating his financial woes that he might have heretofore rejected?

Then there was Bertram, a very dull fellow indeed. Alex doubted that Bertram had all the wits that were commonly bestowed at birth; in any case, he did not reveal evidence of them. He seemed to live only to eat, to read odd books from the library, build houses of cards, and respond to his mother's demands.

Aunt Eliza was an interesting study. *She might be involved in intrigue*, Alex felt wryly, *if she were a man, or some years younger.* She did have Bertram at her beck and call, but even Aunt Eliza knew Bertram's limitations.

Alex was left with his father to consider—and Joanna.

Alex winced as the razor nicked him, and he put down the razor and pressed a cloth on the wound.

Joanna is not capable, he thought. She might feel desperate, but that was not sufficient. Not for Joanna. She was above deception; she would never involve herself in an illegal scheme.

His father was another thing entirely. Alex had come home almost expecting to see his father's mental capacity failing him, but had discovered that this was not the case. His father was as sharp, as cunning, and as mean as he ever had been, and physically he was capable of most any task he set his mind on. But, save for his father's private stash of French brandy, Alex could not see why he would be remotely interested in a smuggling career.

Damnation, he hoped this was true. Alex had got wind of increased smuggling in the area, and had given up his commission so that he would not need to answer to anyone save his own conscience—but his conscience would have something to say about his father's involvement in crimes against the crown.

Alex sighed and picked up the razor. Delicately stroking it along his throat, he thought of Miss MacLaren.

Miss MacLaren—the mouse fallen into the cook pot. She now swam strenuously in the stew, not realizing that defeat was inevitable. She would drown, or be dipped out by an infuriated cook and thrown to the dogs. Regardless of her fate, however, her very presence threw all into turmoil. One was either concerned that she would steal one's inheritance or fearful she would guess one's secrets. Either idea was fodder for hostility against Miss MacLaren.

Alex had to admit that she distracted him. He had already dismissed her owning any criminal tendencies, but might that be due to blindness on his part? He did not know her so very well, even if he had assured himself that she was exactly who she claimed to be.

It was very difficult for him to suspect Miss MacLaren of anything, as a matter of fact. The little he had learned of her in the short time since she had arrived had forcibly changed his initial suspicions. She seemed a sincere, giving, hardworking soul who had more fortitude than common sense. He wondered when his father would tire of her, or whether she would tire of him.

Last night at dinner the vicar had been present as a guest, which, surprisingly enough, was a normal occurrence. One might not suppose Lord Wintercroft and the vicar to be friends; certainly they shared nothing in common. And yet the vicar made his regular calls, and was tolerated by Lord Wintercroft. At least, Lord Wintercroft practiced forbearance during the reverend's visits.

It was during the reverend's visit that Miss MacLaren had announced the need to increase staff. Alex might have expected an explosive reaction from his father, but Lord Wintercroft did not protest. Miss MacLaren had got around him.

Score the first victory to Miss MacLaren. Alex could give her that with equanimity. In the end, Miss MacLaren would lose.

Alex dropped the towel. It was unfortunate that he cared that she *survive*, however. He did not know why he cared, but he did, and those for whom he cared often had a tendency to meet untimely ends. There the matter was. Like it or not, Miss MacLaren's fate was inextricably tied to his own.

Alex turned away from the mirror. This morning he would walk the water's edge and look for signs of activity, as well as check some of the hiding places he knew. With luck he would return before anyone else had stirred from the house.

With any more luck, he would encounter the intriguing Miss MacLaren.

That morning Cora prepared to closet herself with the housekeeper, Mrs. Flynn, to learn how Wintercroft was run. She knew that housekeeping matters were in dire straits, having seen the dust, the dirty carpets, the cobwebs, and the blackened fire grates; but there was still a great deal she needed to know.

Cora also welcomed a distraction from thoughts of Mr. Alex and his surprising behavior the day before. They had accompanied her to bed and greeted her in the morning, with no result other than her original conclusion on the matter: Mr. Alex had either acted from strong concern for her safety or had meant to give her a severe fright. She might have been less confused if it had not been for the vicar's words in favor of him. Clearly there was more to Mr. Alex's character than she knew.

Dressed in a serviceable round gown, Cora arrived at the housekeeper's room at an early hour. Mrs. Flynn invited her in with a nod and a scowl, and indicated that Cora might sit on the one chair. Mrs. Flynn positioned herself before her, her bony hands folded in front of her apron.

The housekeeper was a tall, gaunt woman with protuberant eyes. Her manner was as spare as her appearance. She wore her hair pulled back into a severe gray bun, did not mince words, and did not care who Cora was one way or the other.

"I will not be accused of neglecting my duties," she said by way of a greeting. "I used to have four girls under me, and they did not have to wait table or carry wood. There were two footmen for that. I have two girls now, and one is waiting on you as well. The only menservants in the house are Mr. Potts, who has been laid up with rheumatism and is useless, and his lordship's valet. I have to have the groom draw water!"

Mrs. Flynn stared fiercely at Cora, as though daring Cora to challenge her.

"I see. I thought it was something of the kind. We shall need to hire more help."

Mrs. Flynn hesitated but for the briefest moment then continued her diatribe, her voice only slightly less strident, as though she did not really believe what she had heard.

"There is a great need for more linens. There is no time for proper scouring of things. It is a wonder we are not all eaten alive by bedbugs."

"It seems that Lord Wintercroft has not been eaten alive," Cora replied calmly. "You should have had your help then, I would think." Cora rose to her feet. "Some persons will be coming by to apply for employment, and you may interview them. In the meantime, I will be of some use. I shall begin by sweeping the carpets. That is, unless there is something more urgent that needs to be done."

And so Cora astonished the housekeeper in much the same way she had astonished the cook. She discovered in Mrs. Flynn a very avid cleaning partner, who rejoiced in the prospect of new help by a display of zealous enthusiasm at her job.

Cora was on her knees brushing the drawing room

carpet, her hair under a cap and her dress covered with a stained apron, when Lord Wintercroft strode into the room.

"Stop that and get out!" was his pithy command.

Cora looked up at him. Her hair trailed in her eyes and she was uncomfortably overheated, but the sight of her husband-to-be did not intimidate her.

"Is there a reason this should not be done?" she asked.

Lord Wintercroft blinked, then stared at her as if she were a specter. "Miss MacLaren! What in the name of Almighty God—"

"I am sweeping the carpet." She sat back on her heels and brushed the hair from her eyes, noticing belatedly that her fingers were quite black. "It needs sweeping, you see."

His lordship was so flustered that he stuttered. "It—it is d-done in the afternoon!" he barked.

She looked at him once more and noticed he was a deal paler than she was used to seeing him.

"No, it is not," she said gently. "It has not been done at all."

He took a large breath. Then he took another. "Get up," he snapped, "and get out of that dreadful . . . thing you are wearing! You are not to do such work! You look like a scrubwoman!"

Cora stood and faced him. "That is exactly what I am today. I am determined to live in a properly kept house, and there are matters to be amended. I do not live in dirt."

Lord Wintercroft drew another breath, he stuttered some more, and then he said, "Then you must hire help, not do it yourself! I will not stand for it! Lady Wintercroft does not sweep floors!"

With that, he turned on his heel and, muttering something about a Scotswoman, narrowly missed his son, who was standing in the doorway.

Lord Wintercroft stormed past Alex without a word or notice, but Cora was affected very differently. As she stared at Alex, stilled by surprise, she felt the familiar heat coming over her face—and it was not the heat of exertion.

Alex nodded slightly. "Miss MacLaren," he said. He kept his gaze on her, his dark eyes exploring her dress and then her face.

He wore snug buckskin breeches, boots, and a riding coat, and dangled a beaver top hat from one hand. He was freshly shaved and his hair was neatly combed. This time he had the advantage over her, for she knew she looked her worst.

"I can turn about for your examination, if you like," she said icily.

He raised one brow. "No need. I am yet taking you in from this angle."

There was a change in him—again. It was not that he was neatly dressed, for she had seen him so before. It was not that he had improved in manner, although he had been polite toward her since she had met him yesterday by the cliff.

No, this change was in his eyes. There was a searching in them, a curiosity, and—did she dare believe it?—warmth.

No, that could not be. He could not be looking at her with that kind of feeling. It was preposterous. He found her amusing in this state, perhaps, a reaction she found no more desirable than the first possibility.

She drew a deep breath. "I am sure you have seen all and now are quite as bored as I am. Give me your opinion if you wish. I can withstand any abuse you have to offer, I assure you."

"I have a thought that you can," he said, "but I can add nothing to my father's assessment. I am at an astonishing loss for words." His tone said nothing of disapproval; it might have been teasing had he smiled. It flustered her, and she felt her disadvantage even more keenly.

"Very well, then." She glared at him, hoping her look conveyed all the self-assurance she did not feel. "If you will excuse me, I must finish up."

"I shall go if you wish," he said, and began to turn. Then he paused and cast her a glance over his shoulder. "But I am not at all bored."

Cora had arisen knowing that a full day lay before her, and it invigorated her. Lord Wintercroft was still of the mind to allow her to pursue her improvements, and she meant to make the most of her opportunity before he changed his opinion.

Given the age of the original portion of Wintercroft, the servants' section was constructed in a series of rooms that had been added at various times with little thought to plan. Beyond the original kitchen lay the scullery, the cook's room, the larder, a game larder, and the pantry. Farther down were several other small rooms, interconnected like a spider's web, and a very long underground corridor passing on to a place where wood was stored, although Cora had not traversed that far. There was also Mrs. Flynn's domain, the stillroom, and the laundry, and somewhere in the further depths were the strong room and the wine cellar.

As Cora passed through the kitchen, she was gratified to see Mrs. Potts and Mrs. Mason hard at work in a kitchen that was very much improved from the day before. They exchanged greetings, and Cora continued on to Mrs. Flynn's room. They would complete an inventory of linens and household stores, and Mrs. Flynn would meet with the prospective applicants for employment.

The day passed rather swiftly in these occupations. Cora was thankful to be so busy, and she reflected on this during those little pauses when her mind might be given to wandering to matters other than household affairs. She had a terrible tendency to think of Mr. Alexander, and whenever this happened she felt an uncomfortable tightness in her midsection and a tumult in her mind that was not at all comfortable. It was so much easier to be busy with no room for such reflection. In occupation there was no anxiety, no puzzlement, no useless speculation.

While busy, she could not remember Mr. Alexander's urgent effort to pull her away from the cliff or the look on his face. She could not remember the glint of warmth in his storm-dark eyes, eyes so deep they seemed to see to her soul.

It did her no good to remember those things; thank goodness she was prevented!

It was during one of the painful lulls in her day

that she came into the kitchen to get a cold drink and observe Mrs. Potts instructing the new scullery maid. Mrs. Flynn had gone upstairs with a newly hired housemaid, the inventory was completed, and unwanted thoughts of Mr. Alexander intruded.

She wondered what to think of Mr. Alexander—or Alex, as he was becoming in her thoughts, as he was called by every other member of the household. She thought of the hint of warmth in his eyes for that one moment and the startling line of thought that had come to her—that somehow she had begun to earn his regard.

Which seemed wholly impossible. How could it be otherwise? She might be inclined to forgive him his initial boorish behavior, but she represented a threat to him. He could not possibly admire her if he feared she would steal his inheritance.

"I am not at all bored." He had looked at her so . . . *not at all like a man who was gazing at something he despised. She had looked such a fright, and yet . . .*

Lord! She had to stop thinking these thoughts. And then, as if sent by magic, Lord Wintercroft's valet, Herring, stepped into the kitchen.

"I am in need of beeswax and a good bottle of wine. Where is Mrs. Flynn?"

"She is upstairs," said Cora.

Lord Wintercroft's man looked at her and an expression of surprise came over his face. "I beg your pardon. I did not see you, Miss MacLaren."

"I shall tell Mrs. Flynn what you need when she returns."

"Thank you, miss."

The servant left, and at that moment, Cora remembered that Mrs. Flynn's keys were in her possession. Mrs. Flynn had left them with her before going upstairs. Relieved to have something productive to do, she slipped out of the kitchen and went to the storeroom.

The beeswax was elusive, but Cora persisted until she found it. Locking the storeroom, she next went to the wine cellar.

The old hallway was very still, only faintly lit by a distant window and the candlestick she had brought from the kitchen. Cora tried one key, then another. She was beginning to doubt that Mrs. Flynn had the key at all when one finally turned the lock.

The door opened easily. She stepped into the dark chamber and hesitated, moving her candle about to get her bearings. It was a small room, musty and close, with wooden racks on three walls rising to the ceiling. Cora moved forward slowly, candle foremost, and began examining the dusty bottles. Her foot came down upon something small and hard on the wood floor.

She bent and picked it up. It was a key. It had lain in a space between two shelves, a space large enough for a man to slip through, although there was no reason that one would as the shelves stood against a wall.

She dropped the key in her apron pocket, deciding to ask Mrs. Flynn about it later. And then, in the flicker of candle flame, she noticed a horizontal crack across the boards in the wall. It was just above her own height.

It took her only a moment to discover the narrow door, concealed by the closeness of the shelves. When she found the lock, it was only sensible to try the key.

It fit. Cora pushed the door inward and held out her candle.

The hidden door opened above narrow steps leading downward. Cautiously Cora tried the first step and found it firm. Holding out her candle, she saw that there were only three more steps to the bottom and she glimpsed a large covered object on the floor below.

With Cora, curiosity and determination always overpowered fear. Determined to know what the strange, lumpy thing was, she continued down the steps. She reached the bottom, put down her candlestick, and carefully lifted the corner of a dusty piece of sacking, lest she disturb any small creatures.

She saw the rounded, tarred side of a keg and she knew that it must contain French brandy. There was not only one keg under the sacking, but perhaps four.

Her candle flickered dangerously. Cora dropped the cloth and bent quickly to rescue it, shielding the flame with her hand. A slight gust of air had come from somewhere.

Cora straightened and stood frowning. Then she glanced about herself. This place appeared to be nothing more than a small chamber. A cursory look revealed nothing more, no other door or hallway. The gust had come from above, then.

She turned back to the stairs, wondering what to do about her discovery. It was clearly more brandy than was needed for household use, and it pained her to do nothing. And yet she had no idea who the guilty party was.

She began climbing the steps—and then she saw the candlelight playing against the back of the hidden door.

Someone had closed it.

Chapter Twelve

The assembly in the study was a somber one. Lord Wintercroft sat in his favorite chair by the fireplace, a half-empty wine goblet in hand, glowering from under his thick brows at everyone. Mrs. Flynn, Mrs. Potts, Mrs. Mason, Birdie, and Herring, Lord Wintercroft's personal servant, stood before him. Lounging in the chair opposite Wintercroft was Roland, artlessly examining his fingernails, and in the chair beside him was Robert, properly alert and attentive. Bertram sat beside his uncle, his smooth face unexpressive. Alexander stood behind Bertram, arms crossed, watching intently.

"Mrs. Flynn?" barked Lord Wintercroft.

"I left her in the kitchen, my lord. I went upstairs with one of the new girls."

"Mrs. Potts?"

"I don't know where she is, sir. I was at my work. I didn't see her come nor go."

"You!" Lord Wintercroft glared at Mrs. Mason.

Mrs. Mason curtsied. "Mary, my lord. I did see her

come into the kitchen once, but I did not notice her leave, sir."

"Girl!"

Birdie jumped and said, "I—I l-looked for her. She's g-gone."

"Gone? What in the name of the Almighty is *gone*?"

Birdie covered her face and began to whimper.

Wintercroft turned his eyes on his manservant. "Herring?"

Herring bowed. "She was in the kitchen, sir. I went there to fetch items I needed to polish your boots."

"And when was that?"

"It was past midday, sir."

"Well, where in the devil has she gone?" bellowed Lord Wintercroft.

"I believe," Roland said, "that the life of the future bride of Lord Wintercroft suddenly became less palatable to her. I should think she tossed off her pinafore and abandoned us."

"Shut up, you fool!" said Wintercroft. "When I want your insolence, I shall ask for it!"

"Birdie," said Alex quietly, "where did you expect Miss MacLaren to be?"

Birdie turned wet, beseeching eyes to Alexander. "I—I—"

"Wipe your eyes," Alex said gently. "You did nothing wrong. Tell us what you know."

Birdie sniffed, lifted her apron, and wiped her face with it. Then she took a shaky breath.

"It was time for tea," she said faintly. "I knew she was working downstairs, with the hirin' and all. I waited. Then I looked for her. No one"—her voice trembled—"no one knew . . ."

"You did not expect her to leave? To go anywhere?"

"N-no, sir."

"You cannot think why you could not find her?"

"No, sir."

A silence fell.

"We shall have to look for her," said Robert at last. "We may as well begin. We shall have darkness if we continue to wait."

"*I* shall decide what we are going to do," snapped Wintercroft. He looked at Herring. "Where are my boots?"

Herring cleared his throat. "I shall fetch them, sir. But I was unable to polish them . . ."

"You were *unable* to polish them?"

"I could not get the beeswax and wine—"

Wintercroft uttered a curse and flung his wineglass into the fireplace.

"I am sorry, sir."

"Herring," Alex said, "you wanted beeswax and wine, did you say?"

"Yes, sir."

"Did you tell Miss MacLaren this?"

"I did, sir. She was to tell Mrs. Flynn."

"Well, that would not have helped," Mrs. Flynn snapped, "because she has my keys. I shan't be blamed for it!"

Alex looked at Mrs. Flynn. "Miss MacLaren has your keys?"

"Yes, sir. She was finishing the inventory of linens, so I left them with her."

"She has run off with the bedsheets," said Roland. "I knew it was some such thing!"

"That is enough from you! If you were not my brother's son—"

"Roland, can you not see how serious this is? How can you upset Uncle at a time like this?" Robert said.

Alexander quietly slipped away from the family group as it burst once more into chaos, knowing it would last until he was well out of both sight and mind. Leaving his father's study, he took the stairs down to the ground floor and passed through the new hall into the old part of Wintercroft. He made his way to the old hall, took the servants' hall to the kitchen, and unerringly found his way to the storeroom.

It was unlocked; no one was within.

He went on, following the dark, narrow hall that turned this way and that with no evident reason, and plucked a burning candle from the last sconce as he neared the wine cellar.

He tried the wine cellar door. Oddly, this door was unlocked as well, although closed. Apparently Mrs. Potts and Mrs. Flynn's search for Cora had extended no farther than observing the closed door and assuming it was locked.

He was very concerned now. He opened the door and stepped in, holding the candle high.

Nothing. The room was empty. Unlocked, but empty—and that made no sense, unless the adventurous Miss MacLaren had discovered something she should not have.

With Miss MacLaren, he felt that was entirely possible. But what might she have found? Or, of more concern, who might have seen her?

Alexander knew as few others did the secret of the underground passages at Wintercroft. He had grown up there with too much time to himself, hearing too many stories of ghosts and smugglers from the servants. He did not know every hiding hole and passage at Wintercroft, however. And there was a very good chance that someone else did.

He walked to the center of the room, turning slowly, studying the dusty wine racks and the solid wood paneled walls behind them.

Damn. I should have examined this room before. There, between two large racks, his trained eye detected the faint outline of a narrow door. Then he noted the disturbance of dust on the floor—footprints, handprints—and a small iron key protruding from a concealed lock in the door.

She was down there—and someone knew it!

His heart hammering, he turned the key and pushed the narrow door in. There was no way he could prevent himself from being a target for anyone on the other side; he had to hope there was no need. He ducked to fit his head and shoulders through, then froze, candle in hand.

Below him in the faint halo of candlelight sat a disheveled woman, her eyes closed, her head propped against a rag-covered cache of smuggled brandy.

*   *   *

The rosy glow through her lids startled her to alertness, and she opened her eyes. Hovering very close to hers was the face of a man—a harsh face, a face of strong planes and lines, with very dark, searching eyes.

"Miss MacLaren?"

Alex. Of course, it was Alex. Who but Alex would find her here? As she gazed up at him she became strongly conscious of him kneeling over her, of his presence radiating warmth and surrounding her. She thought of how impressive a form he possessed, how broad of shoulder he was. And she thought of how, incredibly, he made her feel safe.

"Yes, it is I," she said. "Have you come to lead me from the maze again?"

For a heartbeat he looked at her, and then he smiled. His smile grew until his teeth glinted in the candlelight. She stared at him, transfixed at the incredible change in his face.

Alexander was actually quite handsome!

"Miss MacLaren," he said, "you are the oddest sort of female I have ever encountered. Do you fear nothing? You have been shut up in the dark for a good part of the afternoon. I should think I would be discovering a bedlamite."

"Perhaps you have. I have been wondering for some time how I managed to lock myself down here."

His smile faded. "It is no matter, so long as you are not hurt. Are you?"

"Hurt? No, I do not believe so. My pride is injured, that is all."

It was indeed odd how she felt with him now. She had been very afraid before he came, although she would not admit it. She had used her self-command to control her panic and conserve her strength, but it had been exhausting to continually push away the fear and think of other things, especially after the candle had burned out. But now she felt more than relief. She felt happy that it was Alex who had come for her.

"Hold my candle," he said.

She took it, and before she could say a word he had gathered her up and stood with her in his arms.

"But I am quite well! Let me down. I shall do you an injury, I am sure!"

But he was already going up the stair, and she had already found a very comfortable spot on his shoulder for her head.

"I shall have to duck. Watch the candle."

It was a struggle for him to go through the small door with her in his arms, and after two attempts, Cora burst into laughter, and he was forced to let her down onto her own feet again.

"I am sorry," he said. "My best effort to be a hero, and all comes to naught."

She turned to him on the top step. He was bent down so his face was very close to hers, his perplexed expression clear in the candlelight. She grinned up at him. "Ah, but a hero may be many things. You happen to be a large one. I cannot fault you for that."

Then, before she could think any more on it, she raised her face and kissed him gently on the lips.

He went still. She *felt* his body go quiet, as if he were taken aback, and then he pulled away, turned her to face the doorway, and pushed her gently through it.

She turned back to him from the center of the wine cellar and watched him fit his large self through the narrow doorway, not knowing what to say to him or how to explain her behavior. She was always so impulsive when she could least afford to be. As he wedged himself between the two wine racks she was still frantically reviewing possible things to say—and then he was in front of her, gazing down at her face.

"Why did you kiss me?" he asked.

She opened her mouth and found that the right words still eluded her. She licked her lips. "I do not know." She paused. "I wanted to."

He took the candle from her hand and placed it on the near shelf. Then he wrapped his arms around her, drew her very close, and brushed his lips over hers.

She opened her mouth.

He parted his lips and laid them gently over hers. He cupped the back of her head and drew her into his kiss—and Cora felt the sweet, warm wonder of it flow around and through her, dizzying her senses and obliterating all memory.

He drew back slightly. "Miss MacLaren," he whispered, and placed another small kiss on her lips, "are you a dream?" He kissed her once more.

Cora pulled back and stared up at him. "I can quite honestly tell you that I am not."

He looked back for a moment, and then he sighed.

"I was afraid that was so. And now you will no doubt tell me how contemptible I am, and how boorish and unmannered, and I shall creep away growling and snapping to lick my wounds."

Her heart pounded in her neck. She felt weak and shaky. How could she explain to this man why she cared about him when she could not even explain it to herself? And how could he care for her? And even as she thought this, she felt his hands resting warmly on her shoulders.

"I thought you hated me," she said.

"Hate you?" He hesitated. "I have no reason to hate you."

"I cannot believe that."

"I wanted to frighten you away, but only because there is nothing but unhappiness and trouble here."

"Your father means to disinherit you because of me."

"My father does not like me. You have taken nothing from me."

"Why does your father not like you?"

Alexander sighed. "It is no secret. He does not believe I am his son. So you may feel doubly sure that anything he may give to you, or to anyone else, would not have been offered to me."

"Then why did you come back to Wintercroft?"

She felt his gaze intensely in the dark and realized how much her question might have hurt him.

"There are some matters of which I cannot speak."

"Might they concern the kegs of French br—"

"*Hush.*" He squeezed her shoulders. "Perhaps. And it is safest for you not to know."

"I think I must know. I cannot stay without knowing, and I plan on staying here. Tell me now if you have anything to do with the contents of the small room."

He hesitated. "No. I do not. But I mean to learn who does."

"Very well. We can help each other, then."

"No. It is not safe for you. Miss MacLaren, someone deliberately locked you in that room."

Cora took dinner in her room. After her day, she felt in no way able to face the tension and the censorious eyes at the table that night. They would think what they might about her getting locked in the wine cellar—for that was where they thought she had been. Alex had particularly told her not to mention the little room, and she had not done so.

A noticeably happier Birdie brought her tray and informed her that a cousin had applied for employment on that day and been hired by Mrs. Flynn on the spot. Cora felt satisfaction in that, but after Birdie left, her spirits fell. It was because she was weary, she thought, and yet as she parted the draperies in front of a window and gazed out over the dusk-steeped garden, an unmistakable feeling of loneliness overcame her.

She was needed, yes—in her own humble opinion, she was. But wanted? No. Not in the way she wished to be. It seemed that she had put forth a tremendous effort, and yet she sensed that the thing she most desired was not forthcoming.

Alex had kissed her. Alex had opened her eyes.

This was the feeling she had been missing—a feeling of belonging in this life, of companionship, of being truly valued. Of being loved. And yet she had none of these from Alexander. She had only the longing for them he had inspired.

There could be no future for Alexander and her. She had only her heart to offer; he had little more, should he wish to offer it. And, she had to admit, she had little idea that he did.

She should not expect such regard. Her purpose was not to earn gratitude for herself. It was not to win happiness and belonging. And as she gazed outward the shadows blurred, and she saw her father's face and remembered, just for an instant, the feeling of his arm around her as she sat upon his knee.

The shadows in the garden lengthened and darkened, and still she stood gazing out. She could not seem to bring herself to withdraw, not while the peaceful scene lay below backed by the distant glint of the sea.

It was then that she saw her.

The woman stepped out of the maze and paused to glance about. She then hurried toward the house, clutching the dark cape around herself.

Cora had no doubt who it was, even though she could not see the woman's face, nor barely make out her form. She was as sure as she had ever been of anything in her life that the figure was Joanna. But whatever was Joanna doing in the maze in the dusk of evening?

A second movement startled Cora out of her reverie. This time the figure was a man's. He left the

maze as furtively as Joanna had and strode rapidly
away in the direction of the ocean.

He was a tall man in dark garb, and again she saw
little more than that as he blended into the shadows.
But she knew the walk and the characteristic way he
held his head.

The man was Alexander.

Cora dropped the drapery and stepped back. A
lovers' tryst! It could be nothing else. *I cannot marry
my brother-in-law, and you cannot marry your son-in-
law.* Joanna had been much more plain with her than
Cora had realized.

It felt as though there were a gaping wound in
her chest.

Cora turned abruptly from the window, determined to defeat the awful emotion that was welling
within her and return to the rudiments of sanity. But
after pacing in her room for perhaps half an hour,
she had solved nothing, and she had still another
question.

Where had Alex been going?

He had set off in the direction of the cliffs. There
was no reason she could conceive of that would send
him in that direction after an encounter with Joanna.

Unless it had something to do with the contents of
the little room.

For a moment she stood transfixed; then she darted
to her wardrobe and grabbed her day dress from the
hook. Feverishly she donned the gown, fastened
what hooks she could before losing patience and
grabbing her shawl up once more. Friend or foe, she
would learn what Alex was up to!

Chapter Thirteen

Alexander was long out of sight by the time Cora reached the garden. The light was failing now, but the last rays came faintly from the western sky, illuminating her walk to the sea.

The chalk meadow was a barren place, even more so at night. The wind from over the channel whipped at her gown and hair, blowing her cap until it billowed out behind her, moored by its strings. She held her shawl closely about herself and watched the skyline keenly for the silhouette of a man along the high cliff's edge. She saw nothing but the shape of the land against the sea.

As she faced the damp air a memory came, a tune sung softly in her father's voice:

Lonely the wind doth blow o'er the westward sea
Lonely doth the sparrow sing in the boughs of yon-
der tree
And the bluebells nod and shed their tears as I go
wandering by

And I know they mourn for you, my love, they
   mourn for you and I.

Cora smiled to herself, although a tear threatened,
and hummed the chorus softly as the words played
in her head.

Don't you cry, my wee one, my sweet
Your mama with the angels doth keep
The wind that blows o'er the westward sea
Will rock you softly, softly to sleep.

She found herself standing very near the cliff's
edge as the chorus faded in her mind. Here the sea
grass had run into clumps of twisted shrubbery, and
here and there the ground dipped. There were a few
large cracks in the earth, as well as bits of the cliff
that seemed on the verge of falling into the sea. Beyond and far below, the sea had turned a steely blue,
soon to become the black of night.

Cora sighed. She would not find Alexander here.
She would find nothing here. He had told her one
thing at least that was right: there was nothing but
unhappiness and trouble in this place.

Did she have the heart to work on, to heal the
trouble here, when there would be only heartbreak
for her? For as certain as anything was she that she
had fallen in love with the black sheep of
Wintercroft.

Ah, but the sea was truly beautiful.

Cora found a snug spot by a clump of shrubbery
where the ground sloped downward, and sat down

on a flat stone. Here in shadow, protected from the worst of the wind, she tucked her feet under her skirt and watched the inky darkness fall over the water.

Perhaps she *should* marry Lord Wintercroft. Perhaps staying here would afford her the chance to help others that she otherwise would never have. Was that not her purpose? Should she abandon such a chance? A chance to create work, to bring a doctor to the village, to support the good work of the parish?

There was nothing to say that Lord Wintercroft would continue to let her have her way; there was all likelihood that he would close his purse to her one day if he kept to his old habits. Still, she felt her ability gave her a chance to reform the clutch-fisted old fox. She simply needed to convince him that her way would make him happy.

Cora sighed. There were serious matters to be resolved first, however, not the least of them the matter of the illegal brandy at Wintercroft. It was so very odd, though; she could not see how the brandy had come to be in the little room—or how it would leave. It had hardly been carried through the halls of Wintercroft!

It was now nearly full dark. Even with her eyes attuned to the darkness, she would have difficulty finding her way, but she had no fear of that. This peace that she felt at the edge of the sea was well worth the price.

She sighed and laid her hand on the earth beside her. She felt her fingers come in contact with something flat and smooth.

It was perfectly oval, and it glimmered in the darkness. Cora turned the object over and over in her hands. It was silver, and she felt a tiny latch. A snuffbox.

She was intrigued and looked forward to examining it more closely. For now she slipped it into her pocket, wondering what sort of gentleman had dropped it.

It was then that she saw the flash of blue light in the dark void of water.

She stared outward, thinking that she had perhaps imagined it. Then she saw it again—a blue light. First it was there and then it was not.

A signal.

Her walk to the sea had not been for naught after all. Here was something to investigate, but she was so ill prepared to do so! Her shoes were not fit for anything but the most gentle path or field. She longed for her warm cloak, and it was too dark to mind one's footing as one should. Still, she got to her feet, keeping low, and followed the edge of the cliff as it sloped toward the beach.

Alexander must have known about this. There was no other reason he would have walked this way. If so, he had lied to her—and he had kissed her when he meant to keep an assignation with Joanna! *There is a lesson to you. Why must I be so blessed impulsive?*

She had reached a place where the cliff was much closer to the water and the chalk face more gradual, making it possible to walk down the slope if one were careful. She started a cautious descent. The light-colored stone reflected the available light, making it possible for her to find her way, placing a foot there, her hand here for balance, her other foot there. *Just a little farther and I will be able to see where the boat comes to shore.* Once she could see around the protruding face of the cliff she would have a straight line of sight to the water's edge for a good distance, all the way to Birling Gap.

She gazed out at the water, straining for a sight of the blue light. Although it should be visible to her again, it did not reappear. Still looking, she reached for her next step, and her shoe slid on a loose stone.

In lightning sequence she lost her purchase and fell backward, and all was punctuated by the rattle of falling stone. She sat still, her bottom hurting and her heart racing.

Oh, my Lord. I should never have done this.

It was very late to be having that thought. She was now halfway down the cliff face, and her presence had been well announced. Anyone on the beach who did not wish to be discovered now knew there was a watcher.

Should she stay still? Climb up? She moved her hand and her upper arm throbbed dully. She drew a breath and slowly moved one leg, biting her lip when the same throbbing pain began in her hip. She was at last able to rise to her feet on the rocky slope. Slowly, she began to climb.

If Lord Wintercroft were to see me now, I should no longer need to be concerned about marrying him.

The idea suddenly seemed so ridiculous that she nearly burst out in a laugh. It had to be due to pain or fear, she thought. She was losing her slim grasp on sanity.

A shadow appeared from behind an outcropping of rock.

She froze. In the next instant the man was beside her, his hard arm tight around her middle, his gloved hand over her mouth.

"Be quiet," he whispered.

She went still. She felt the warmth of his body, the beat of his heart, the brush of his breath on her cheek.

Alexander.

He said nothing for a long moment, but she realized his attention was not on her. He seemed to be listening . . . watching.

"There are men on the beach and they have heard you," he whispered. "We must move from here."

She tried to speak, and he moved his hand.

"That is what I was trying to do," she whispered back. "You are crushing the breath out of me."

"I am sorry, to be sure." He relaxed his arm. "Come." He turned toward the sea, still holding her closely to his side, and began compelling her downward.

"Why are we going down?"

"Trust me."

"This is a fine time to tell me that!"

"Quiet, please! And hurry."

The descent would have been manageable in daylight by a fit person in proper shoes; Cora had neither proper shoes nor light. But Alex was strong and determined, and he kept his arm snug around her. He clambered down the slope at breakneck speed, holding her when she slipped, taking her with him.

They reached the bottom, a small slide of stone accompanying them.

"You are mad!" she whispered breathlessly.

"I have been accused of worse."

From farther up the beach came the sound of a man's shout.

"This way!" Alex said urgently. Turning north, he began to run, pulling her with him.

She tried to look back. There was a light far down the beach—a bouncing, moving light. They were being chased.

"Here—*quickly!*" Alex pulled her behind a mound of stone. A shot rang out.

"Alexander—"

"Quiet!"

"I shall never forgive you!"

"Never will be very short unless you are quiet!"

He pulled her onward. They were entering a kind of crack in the face of the cliff, a crevice in the chalk with jagged walls of it about them. She could see the white of the stone glowing softly; where it was not was only blackness.

"What is this?"

"Just come with me."

The rock closed overhead, and suddenly they were in total darkness.

"Alex, I do not like this!"

"Hold my hand and follow me."

"Whom are *you* following?"

"I can feel my way. Do not distract me."

"I believe I have not a prayer of distracting you."

"Watch your step. The ground can be uneven."

"Ugh! I have stepped in water."

"As have I."

"Is this a cave?"

"Yes, my dear, it is. Once, it was a *quiet* cave."

Cora stopped talking. She had no choice but to follow him, and she preferred that the men on the beach did not do so as well. But her heart beat rapidly, her feet were bruised and hurt in her useless flat shoes, and they had got wet besides.

The cavern they were in seemed to grow smaller as they proceeded. Cora could feel the walls closing in around them, and a damp chill began to penetrate her bones. Alex kept up an urgent pace, but she sensed his alertness, his complete attention to his task.

"This way. You must duck low. I shall be right behind you. The floor slopes upward—take care not to slip."

"I shall expect a full explanation for this."

"Please, Miss MacLaren." She received a less than gentle push on the rump.

The smaller passage grew even tighter, until Cora was forced to her knees. She stopped.

"Go on," Alex said.

"I cannot. It is shrinking!"

"It is large enough. You can crawl, Miss Mac-Laren."

"Have you ever attempted to crawl in a damp gown?"

"My dear, this is hardly the time for levity."

"Really, sir? I am so amused I can barely contain myself."

"Go *on*, Miss MacLaren!"

Cora began to creep, a great deal more frightened than she allowed Alexander to know. She began to use the trick she had used in the hidden room, pushing the terror into a corner of her mind and thinking of anything else. This proved very hard when one's hands, as well as one's knees, were scraped and raw and when one had to stop frequently and adjust one's skirts.

Then, suddenly, she felt openness and air.

"At last," Alex said. "Now we need to climb just a bit more, and we will be snug as bugs."

"I do not wish to be like a bug. What is this place?"

"A cavern. It is higher than the previous one. You may stand now, but take care with your head. It is still low in places."

She stood, carefully, and raised her head. She felt a breath of moving air.

"Is this the way out?"

"No. It is where we are hiding."

She would have stared at him if she could have seen him. As it was, she could only consider his tone of voice. He sounded serious.

"Hiding? But what if we are followed? If you know of this place, then so do *they*."

"That is likely true. But they will not search for us in here. At least, I hope they will not."

"You *hope* they will not?"

Cora was near trembling with fatigue and chill,

and now fear was escaping that corner of her mind. Perhaps Alexander was mad.

"Pray follow me for a bit more and I will explain."

"I should like it explained now, if you please."

"I would truly like to, but I do not wish for our feet to get more of a wetting. Take my hand."

He grasped her wrist firmly and began to pull her along behind him.

"Why should our feet become wetter?"

"It is just a bit farther. Watch your step—we are climbing now. Stay close to the wall."

Cora's feet encountered an upward grade. Alex continued to pull her along, now at a cautious pace. She reached behind her and felt the damp wall of stone.

"Keep close behind me. The path is narrowing."

Cora tested each step carefully as Alex slowed. Her heart hammered.

"Here we are."

He assisted her in her last two steps and then stopped.

"It is a shelf of sorts. It is big enough to lie upon, and it is no more than a few paces wide. Now, my dear, you may rest."

Cora took a deep breath. "Is the tide coming in?"

He hesitated, and this made her even more afraid of the answer.

"Yes. But we are safe."

She let her breath out and sank down, and he sat with her, still holding her hand.

"How do you know we are safe?" she asked.

"I was born here. A boy learns these things."

"You were never in this cave as a boy. And if you

were, you would not have known what the tide does
when it comes in."

"I do know, Miss MacLaren. You will have to
have faith."

"The men following us will know we are trapped."

"Likely. As I said, I hope they will not follow."

"Because they know we will die."

"We will not die, my skeptical Miss MacLaren. As
for the men, they have better things to do than to
search a cave when the tide is coming in. And if they
believe we shall not survive, then it is so much the
better for us."

She began to shiver in earnest. In response, he removed his coat, draped it around her shoulders, and
drew her close to his side.

"You will catch a chill now," she said.

"I do not catch chills."

She sighed and rested her head upon his shoulder.
It felt the natural thing to do, and she was filled with
a sense of peace.

"Tell me how you know about this cave," she said.

He was quiet a moment. When at last he spoke,
his voice was quiet and thoughtful.

"My mother died shortly after my brother, Arthur,
was born. My father was not fond of me even when
I was very young, and my mother's passing made
matters more difficult. I was a rather difficult child,
I admit. Rather than be ignored, I did things that
guaranteed that I would not be."

"What did you do?"

"I put a snake in the laundry. I let out the dogs. I
threw stones at the fowl."

"That was all very bad."

"It was not the worst. I tarred and feathered my father's boots."

"You did not!"

"I assure you, I did. And that also is the reason I know about this cave. My father made me spend the night here to think about what I had done."

Pain welled within her heart for the poor lost boy. How could he have borne it?

She reached over and gently placed her hand upon his arm. "Poor Alexander," she said.

She felt him stiffen slightly, and he was silent.

"That was a terrible thing for your father to do to you, no matter what you had done."

"I deserved it."

"No, you did not. How old were you? Fifteen?"

"I was twelve years old."

Cora sighed deeply. "Alexander, no matter what has happened between your father and yourself, he was very wrong to treat you so."

"My father knew that I had acted out of anger and spite. He had just given Arthur a chestnut foal, and I wanted it."

"Had you one also?"

"No. But recall that I am another man's son."

"It was a bad thing for him to have done, all the same. You are his heir, and his son in all ways that matter."

Alexander shrugged. "It matters very much to men."

"But you might have drowned!"

"Not at all." He paused, and she felt all the emotion in it. "He knew I would be safe in this cavern, and so he told me. I had only to wait until he came for me. And that, Miss MacLaren, is why I know the tide will not reach us here."

"And this is why your father and you are at such odds always?"

"There are other reasons. It did not help that I am the son to survive."

Cora fell silent. She listened to Alexander breathe and wondered if they could truly escape. What if Lord Wintercroft had *not* known for certain if his son would be safe in this cavern? Or perhaps he had felt certain of it, but what if he had been wrong?

She thought she heard the sound of water coming closer.

"Tell me about Arthur," she said.

"Handsome and spoiled," Alexander said.

"There is more to say than that."

"A good deal, I am afraid, but I am not the one to tell it. He was an engaging child, and one my father was certain belonged to him. I wished I was everything he was and could not be."

"You wanted to be married to Joanna."

He sighed heavily. "Miss MacLaren, you may have me trapped here, but do not expect too much! I am hardly about to discuss my brother's wife with you."

"Tell me of your wife, then. Were you in love with her?"

She knew she heard water now, soft swells of it against stone.

"No. Let that be an end to it."

She said nothing more and was surprised when he spoke again.

"She was a mill owner's daughter. I had my future title, and she had a respectable dowry. It was a matter of convenience between us."

"I am sorry for your loss," she said gently. "I know you must have cared for her."

He drew a heavy breath. "I do not know with whom you have been speaking, but I did not cause my wife's death. She died of a fever. As far as my brother's death, I did not cause that, either. He was in his cups and fell. Does this answer all the questions you have?"

Cora lifted her head from his shoulder, tugged her hand from his, and stood.

"What are you doing?" he asked.

"I am moving, thank you. You may keep your bitterness there; I have quite enough to be concerned with." She stepped away from him.

"Miss MacLaren, do not—"

"If I thought you a murderer, would I be acting as I have?"

He stood and caught her arm. "The edge is near. I will not have you go tumbling off in the dark."

"Of course not. Everyone will believe you pushed me."

"No, it is because I do not *want* you to fall."

They stood together facing each other on the ledge. Cora felt her heart begin to tremble.

"Neither do I want anyone to say ill of you," she said at last.

"Let us rest, then. The tide is still rising. It will be a good while yet before we can leave."

Chapter Fourteen

*C*ora thought she heard the water flowing into their cavern, but it was so very silent she was not certain. Alexander, leaning back against the wall, sat beside her and she thought that perhaps he had fallen asleep.

She found a small stone and closed her fingers around it. A thought struck her, and she felt about and found two other stones, all of which she pocketed. Then she crawled carefully to the lip of the ledge they were on.

Seating herself there, she fished one stone out of her pocket. Holding it aloft, she uttered a silent prayer and let it drop.

Splash.

She let her breath out. Indeed, their chamber was flooded. The level was below that of this ledge, but she wondered how much higher it would rise.

"Miss MacLaren? Where are you?"

"I am right here."

"Come away from the edge."

"I am checking for water in the cavern."

"Come here and sit down. *Now.*"

He sounded genuinely frightened for her. Cora felt a pang of guilt.

"Very well. But I was only dropping stones. Listen." She let another one drop. "You can hear the splash."

She heard him suck in a breath. "I heard it. Now, please come and sit here so I know where you are."

She crept back to his side and sat close to him. She noticed he was quite tense. "Are you cold? You may have your coat."

"I am not cold."

She considered. "You are not certain how high the water will rise, are you?"

"I am certain."

She found his forearm with her hand. "Then why are you so afraid?"

"I am not afraid, Miss MacLaren. I have looked death in the face. I am surely not afraid of sitting in a dark cave for several hours."

"That is certainly a logical thought. But perhaps what you feel defies logic."

"Miss MacLaren, stop attempting to understand me."

"I am not attempting to understand you, but I cannot help but understand some things without trying." She gave his arm a little squeeze.

"You cannot understand something that is beyond your experience."

"Well, I understand being afraid of being trapped in a dark cave with the tide flowing in. Many would be frightened witless. However, I have this odd ability to control my fear. My father always told me I must have either been a Roman centurion in the past—or he was father to the most remarkable young lady alive.''

''However remarkable you are, please humor me and do not venture close to the edge again. And do not try to descend. You would slip and be drowned.''

She settled her hand over his. ''I am afraid, too,'' she said. ''But my father did not force me to spend the night in here when I was twelve years old.''

She felt his body stiffen, and she leaned over and put her arms around him. ''All will be well,'' she said. ''We just need to wait.''

She dreamed she was in a dinghy floating in an endless blue sea. The swells were gentle, rocking her little craft, and the sun was warm on her face. She gazed at the sky above her and saw no birds, only more blue, as if there were nothing in the world but her small boat.

Her feet were cold, however. As warm as the sun was, her feet would not get warm, and when she looked down at them at last, she discovered she was up to her ankles in water.

She opened her eyes.

The sun was gone. It was as black as a mountain of coal. The moment her panic began to rise, she remembered—they were in the cave.

The warmth on her face was Alexander's breath.

In fact, all of her was warm where she lay snuggled up to his big body. Only her feet were cold, as

Alexander's coat was not long enough to cover them. His arm lay over her, heavy and comforting, and she lay very still to savor the painful sweetness of it. Soon enough he would awaken.

She wondered if the water had receded. Thank the Lord, Alex had been right; she was certain they would be drowned by now if he had not been.

Alex stirred and moaned softly. Cora sighed, pulled gently away from him, and sat up. She preferred this memory to be hers alone.

"Miss MacLaren?"

"I am none other."

He sat up beside her and rubbed his head. "I believe I slept. How was it possible that I slept?"

"You were weary?"

"I had no right to sleep. I needed to keep watch."

"Neither of us can see anything. There would not have been much point in that."

"We might have been followed. And the water was rising. I cannot believe that I slept."

"No one could have followed us, and there was nothing you could have done about the water."

"Stop being so blessed logical, Miss MacLaren."

She laughed, and it echoed throughout the cavern.

"God Almighty! Someone may be outside waiting for the tide to recede! You might endeavor to be quiet!"

"They are waiting only if they expect us to be alive, and I wonder how many know one can survive in here? It must be a brave soul to attempt to discover the truth."

"Very well. You have won, Miss MacLaren. I am

an utter fool and you are an indomitable intellect. Now let us decide what we shall do."

Cora thought that there was nothing *logical* about how she was feeling right now. Soon they would be safe and sound and she would never again share intimate hours with Alexander—hours during which they had learned so much about each other and she had fallen deeply, hopelessly, in love.

"I expect we should see if the water is gone, and then walk out of the cavern," she said.

"Excellent. But it is not as simple as all that."

"How so?"

"We have just spent several hours confined in each other's company. There are issues of propriety."

She wished she could see his face, for she could not guess if he was bluffing or telling the truth.

"I hardly think that it matters. First, I am engaged to be married to your father. Second, there is no reason for the world to know about our little incident. Surely we can return to Wintercroft without alerting everyone."

"That may be, but it may not be. Neither of us knows what o'clock it is. We may have passed the entire night here and have been missed."

"We shall learn soon enough. Until then I see no reason for inordinate concern. I would much prefer that no one learn of this, of course. Particularly your father—he will be happy with neither of us."

"Miss MacLaren. Let me speak." He paused. "I think that perhaps you should consider the need . . . the possible need . . . of marrying me."

Cora was entirely wordless. *Marry her? Was it possible that he had actually suggested marriage?*

"Consider the circumstances. My father may prove unwilling to go forward with your marriage plans. In which case, I am your remaining choice." He paused. "Do you not have something to say?"

Cora might have dreamed of a proposal and all the circumstances that would make life with Alexander possible. But the circumstances were *not* present, and Alexander had not said that he loved her. And to Cora, the reason why was perfectly clear.

Cora drew a deep breath. "Only that I never have only *one* remaining choice. I can go my own way, and you need not be troubled with me at all."

He sighed. "I did not speak of *trouble*, Miss MacLaren. I made an offer. And in case you are concerned with my financial status, I admit I am not well set, but I am not a pauper, either. We would live modestly, of course."

"Of course. And would you expect to remain here?"

"I should try to convince my father to allow us to stay. It would be preferable from a practical standpoint."

"And from a social standpoint as well, no doubt."

"What do you mean?"

"I mean you might have your wife and your . . . your *affaire de coeur* under the same roof! But I should not be in favor of that, I am afraid."

"Miss MacLaren, that is the most absurd thing I have ever heard! I do not have any such entanglement!"

He sounded angry now. His anger, and his denial, made her hurt flame into anger. Cora rose to her feet.

"I should like to see if we could leave. If we are fortunate at all, everyone will be asleep!"

"Miss MacLaren, I insist that you explain yourself. With whom are you accusing me of having an affair?"

"Well, it certainly is not with your aunt Eliza!"

"That is in no way helpful."

"Lead the way. I am too distraught to talk about it."

"I disagree. Being distraught does not in the least inhibit your tongue."

"I am speaking of Mrs. Neadow. Mrs. *Arthur* Neadow! Now you may be happy and take me from here at once!"

"I am not having an affair with Joanna."

Not having an affair with Joanna? How dare he deny it! Cora might lack in certain worldly experience, but she was no fool.

"No? Did you meet by chance in the maze, then? You forget that my window is above. So now that this little discussion is over, I wish to leave this cave!"

"Miss MacLaren, I have *not* been meeting Joanna in the maze, or in trees, or in foliage of any kind. I have certainly never met her in a cave! Whoever you saw, it was not me."

Cora sniffed contemptuously. At least, she hoped it *sounded* like a contemptuous sniff. She had no desire for him to guess it was a miserable one.

"Then it was not you whom I saw leave the maze tonight by stealth and depart in the direction of the sea? But how odd—you *did* appear at the cliff tonight, and I have not the faintest idea why."

"I was investigating, just as—I suppose—you were."

"Very well, then. I am satisfied. Please lead me out of here."

She had made certain that her voice conveyed how very dissatisfied she was, and at last he had heard enough.

"Take my hand, then. And do not distract me. If you do, I shall not be held responsible for where we find ourselves!"

The pale rose of dawn softened the sky above the cliff. The water was calm, and the narrow beach looked pure and peaceful in the gossamer mist of the coming morning.

Cora walked up the rise at the low end of the cliff with Alexander behind her. It was a great deal easier to make the climb this morning when she could see where every stone and shale outcropping lay, but it was not the least bit comfortable with Alexander following so close behind her.

She was not so very angry with him as she had caused him to believe. She had reacted in defense of her heart. But in spite of her upset, she held him blameless for where his had led him. She only wished he had not bowed to the temptation and kissed her so very thoroughly in the wine cellar. That was one of those unfortunate things that came with courage; she had wanted to be kissed, and so she had invited him to do so.

She was a little angry, though. One could not be completely above emotion. And she was very, very unhappy. How could she marry Lord Wintercroft? But how could she not marry him now, unless he refused her? For in spite of what she had told Alexander, she did not want to leave with the hint of scandal following her. It would mean her destruction.

They walked over the damp sea grass, past the pretty clumps of yellow gorse and purple heather wearing their veils of dew. Wintercroft rose in the distance, its ancient towers striking against the backdrop of blush-colored sky. But for Cora there was no delight to be had, and she guessed there was none for Alexander, who walked in stony silence at her side.

"I shall enter by way of the kitchen," she said.

"The kitchen fire is lit."

Cora had seen the thin rise of smoke from the kitchen chimney as well, but she would have to risk being seen by Mrs. Potts or one of the other servants.

"The staff has seen me appear worse."

Alexander looked at her, and she felt his penetrating gaze. "No, they have not."

Cora raised her chin. "Shall it be the front door, then?"

"No, not unless we enter it together. And it might be well that we did, for it will be guessed that you have entered by stealth if you pass through the kitchen. At least if we enter by the front door, it is possible we may slip through unseen. It is early still."

It was the front door that they approached, then, in hopes that they might open it to an empty foyer. But as Alexander stood with his hand outreached, the door opened on its own. There, in his powdered wig and somewhat rumpled coat, stood the short, stocky form of Mr. Potts, husband of the cook and the previously ailing butler to Wintercroft.

"Potts! Whatever are you doing out of bed?" exclaimed Alexander.

Potts raised his dignified jowls and gazed at Alexander with that blank butler's expression. "I am better today, thank you, sir. I see that you have returned from a . . . stroll."

Cora, who stood behind Alexander, cleared her throat at this point and stepped into view. "We have both returned from a stroll, Potts. It is lovely this time of morning."

In spite of his schooling, Potts' eyes bulged behind his spectacles. "Of—of course! Lovely! If one does not mind the wind. May I take your coat, Mr.—" Potts had extended his hand toward Alexander, and immediately noticed that Alex was not wearing his coat. Mr. Potts turned to Cora, who was. "Miss MacLaren?"

"Perhaps you might have it cleaned for him," Cora said, and turned so Potts could retrieve the coat from her shoulders.

"Please send Miss MacLaren breakfast in her room," Alexander said. "And send her maid." He lowered his head and said into her ear, "Go *quickly*, if you please."

Cora felt all the urgency of gaining her room quickly, and lost no time yielding Alex's coat to Potts, but there their luck ran out.

"What in thunder is all *this*?"

Halfway down the stairs stood Lord Wintercroft, gripping the banister with one hand and brandishing an ivory-headed cane with the other.

"They have returned from a morning stroll, sir," said Potts.

"Potts, get your empty skull out of my way! Morning stroll! Good Lord, they have spent the night in a ditch somewhere! Look at the mad Scotswoman! She has hair like a bedlamite!"

"Father, this may all be explained."

"You may bet your last boot nail it can be! Into my study with the both of you. Now!"

Cora preceded the men into the study, feeling very grim indeed. It seemed quite certain that her plans for Wintercroft were dashed. All those who had counted upon her—Mrs. Potts, Mrs. Flynn, Birdie, the new staff—would soon learn that their hopes had been for naught. As for the rest, they would remain trapped in this house of pain.

Cora seated herself and was still attempting to straighten her bedraggled skirts when Lord Wintercroft roared out his first accusation.

"Do you two think to make a laughingstock of me?"

"No, Father. The circumstances are somewhat different. We—"

"I am no fool! *You*, sir," Lord Wintercroft shouted, pointing a gnarled finger at Alexander, "meant to steal the march on me with my future bride! And *you*, you—you progeny of Ermintrude—"

"Father, I will not hear you speak so to Miss MacLaren! She has done nothing to deserve this!"

"I will speak how I like! She is engaged to me, or do you forget?"

"It matters not. She will now marry me, and you can have nothing to say about it! It appears that you have your mind made up about us, so there is nothing more to discuss!"

Lord Wintercroft swore and, nearly dancing with fury, grabbed up his cane and waved it at Alexander, forcing Alexander to retreat several steps. "That is where you are *wrong!* She will marry *me*, as planned, and you may stew in your own juice! No bastard living under my roof is going to steal my bride away from me!"

Cora stood. "Stop it!" she shouted.

She was completely ignored. The two now circled each other, Lord Wintercroft threateningly, Alexander warily keeping his distance, and the words continued to fly.

"Miss MacLaren will decide for herself," Alexander said. "She cannot possibly decide upon a bilious old windbag who cannot be bothered by anyone's welfare but his own!"

"Bilious windbag? Do you realize to whom you are speaking?"

"Perfectly, and for the first time I am willing to declare it to all. You are a bilious old windbag who is not my father! I owe you nothing. You have made it perfectly clear that I am but a worthless stone around your neck. You wished me to the devil upon birth. I am now obliging you! I shall be all you accuse me of, and worse!"

Cora arose and started for the door.

"Ingrate! Judas! Bastard of who knows who! Get out of my house! Get out before I—"

Cora turned at the doorway and took one last look at the embattled father and son.

"It is now over," she shouted.

She was surprised when they both stopped speaking and stared at her. Lord Wintercroft's face was ruddy with exertion; Alexander's was as white as chalk.

"I shall marry neither of you. There, it is settled. Make what amends you can. I will not be part of this madhouse."

She stepped out of the study and shoved the door shut behind her. It closed with a decisive thud. She took seven steps up the hall toward the stairs and suddenly sagged to one side and braced her hand against the wall. Her heart pounded and she was trembling.

To the devil with them. To the devil with them all. I cannot help them. I cannot even help myself.

She caught her breath, but a wrenching sob broke forth.

She had to leave. But Alexander . . . oh, Alexander . . .

She fled up the stairs, knowing she must act with all speed before her heart destroyed her resolve.

Chapter Fifteen

"My dear, my poor dear! What has happened to you?"

Cora stepped through the vicar's doorway and promptly fell into his arms, sobbing as if her heart would break.

"Mrs. Cooper! Mrs. Cooper! Come here. I need you."

Cora barely noticed being turned over to the housekeeper and led to the parlor. Soon, though, she was lying on the settee, covered with a warm throw and propped comfortably with pillows, with both Mrs. Cooper and Reverend Nye hovering over her with tea and offerings of toast.

"Come, tell me what has happened," said Reverend Nye.

Cora drew a shuddering breath. "Forgive me. I fear I am weary. I must tell you, however, that I am done with Wintercroft. I have left that place and I cannot return to it. I have failed everyone. Those I have hired will be let go, and Lord Wintercroft and

Alexander hate each other more than ever. And it is all because of me!"

Slowly, between sips of tea and bites of toast, Cora told the whole of it to Reverend Nye while he sat by quietly and sympathetically, saying all that was kind and soothing.

"You alone were not capable of working a miracle there," he said. "The state of things, such as they are, has been so for a long time. As far as the activities you ventured to discover—it is best that you are far from that as well. Would you not agree, Mrs. Cooper?"

Mrs. Cooper shook her head. "You should never have tried to learn nothing about that," she said. "Best left alone. Only bad comes from knowing about what men do at night."

Cora took another breath. "I need a position. I need a place to go. I hoped you could help me, Reverend Nye."

He was quiet a moment, and took that time to refill her teacup.

"Yes, and so I shall. I told you to come to me if you were in trouble, and you did just as you should." He paused. "You may stay here, Miss MacLaren. I do have Mrs. Cooper, of course, but the village needs a good nurse, and the good nurse needs a home. And . . ." He looked at her, his pale blue eyes soft with concern, and she noted the fine lines of worry around them.

"And—I am in need of a wife."

Cora blinked. She scarcely felt anything; he was the third man in a day who had expressed a desire to marry her, after all. But she did sense something new. Tempering the grief was a feeling of peace.

"Would you truly wish to marry me, Reverend Nye?"

"Very much."

It was that simply done. Cora had her answer. She had her place of safety, and a place where she could be of service to others.

"Then I should be honored."

"Thank you, my dear." The reverend rose. "Mrs. Cooper will take care of you. I have some business to attend to. Please make yourself at home—for this *is* your home now."

After Reverend Nye left, Cora leaned back on the pillows, trying to comprehend all that had happened to her. A few hours ago, she had been in a black cavern with her arms around her brave Alexander— for he was indeed the bravest of men. She had realized that as she held him in her arms to comfort him. No man but a brave one would lead her into the cavern to save her when the cavern was the thing that frightened him most. And Cora thought of the father who had subjected a child to such terror— even if he believed the child was not his own.

Something about the recent venture had been freeing for Alexander, though, and she was sorry to see that this had led to his bold tongue-lashing of Lord Wintercroft. For what might have been gained, she had left the family worse off than before.

Now she was to marry Reverend Nye, and undoubtedly in very short time. How would she feel being married to this gentle older man when Alexander's home lay only an hour's walk away? But likely Alexander would not remain at his childhood home, and just as likely she would never see him again.

Restless, she sat up and tossed aside the throw. Her thoughts would simply not allow her to lie still. She placed her feet on the floor of Reverend Nye's charming sitting room and smoothed her skirts—and ran her fingers over something hard in her pocket.

The box.

She had forgotten the box. Impatiently, she pulled it from her pocket and examined it closely.

It was very old, made of wrought silver, with very fine craftsmanship. An intricate design was etched around its edges, and in the center were three initials. She found the catch, and the box opened. It contained a small amount of snuff, which she found disagreeable, and she closed it again.

She studied the initials. The box was worn and scratched, the letters difficult to make out. She puzzled at them for a few moments and suddenly she understood what they were. *ACN. Alexander Chatham Neadow.*

She stared at the initials until they blurred, and then she let the box rest in her lap.

It was Alexander's box. He had been at the cliff before she had arrived. But she had known that. Still, the pain was fresh again, and she had to wonder if Alexander was indeed investigating the activities on the coast—or if he was in fact involved with them.

He had admitted he was poor. His father had made it clear that Alex was to get no money from him. Might Alexander look for fortune from the sea?

On the other hand, was there anyone at Wintercroft who did not have cause to do the same, except Lord Wintercroft himself?

But it had been Alexander who had found her in the little room where the kegs were hidden. Alexander had told her that someone had locked her into the room. Might it just as well have been Alexander himself? If so, when he came to rescue her he would seem innocent, and the danger of her prying where she ought not would have been made clear in her mind.

It had also been Alexander who had pulled her away from the cliff's edge that day, but Cora had never seen the approaching man he had stated he had seen. Alexander had been strange, quiet, brooding, and had even admitted to trying to frighten her away.

Cora held the box so tightly her knuckles hurt, but when Mrs. Cooper swept back into the room, Cora's mind was made up.

"Mrs. Cooper, I have accidentally come away with Alexander Neadow's snuffbox. Can you help me? I must send it back to him and I should like to write him a note."

"Of course, miss. I will fetch Reverend Nye's writing box. One of my boys can deliver the thing for you."

Once left alone with the writing box, Cora began to write, with much hesitation and thought.

Dear A,

I had forgotten to return this to you. As you can see, it is your snuffbox, which I discovered on the cliff

*before you came upon me. I had not thought to exam-
ine it until now and so I am returning it.*

*Do not be concerned for me. I have come to Rever-
end Nye's home and he has generously offered to be
my husband. This suits me quite well, I assure you,
and will hopefully make matters a bit easier to bear
at Wintercroft.*

She hesitated, wanting to say a great deal more,
but knowing that saying too much was unwise. At
last she wrote:

*I bid you farewell, my friend. I hope in my heart that
you make peace with your father, for I do not believe
he hates you as much as you believe.*
All happiness to you,
CM

"Come, my dear. Allow me to show you my humble home. I believe you will find it very comfortable
and welcoming."

It was late in the day of Cora's arrival. She had
rested and restored herself and changed into a clean
gown from the one bag she had brought with her.
She had shared a modest meal with the reverend,
and really did feel very much better. However, she
was not content.

Most of her precious few belongings were still at
Wintercroft, a small matter for the most part, but she
wanted to have her father's medical instruments. She
had conveyed this to the reverend, and he had reassured her and had offered the little tour of his home.

"It is nothing like Wintercroft, but it is a very good home. I am quite proud of it. My father was vicar before me, so you see I am quite attached to it, and also to the community. I was born in a little room upstairs."

Cora replied appropriately as he showed her his neat little rooms. The home was flint-faced and whitewashed, as were the other cottages, but it was larger than most and furnished sparingly but well. It had a small dining room, the luxury of a separate sitting room that doubled as the reverend's study and receiving room for members of his flock, and upstairs, he said, were two small bedrooms.

They began to ascend the stairs. Reverend Nye paused and pointed to a small portrait, halfway up the staircase, of an older gentleman in clerical robes. "My father," he said. "I also have a miniature of my mother in my bedchamber. And here . . ." He mounted several more steps, and Cora followed. "Here is my grandfather! His is quite the tale, and although he is hardly the ancestor for a vicar such as myself, I am inordinately proud of him."

Cora stopped before the portrait and gazed up at it. It was quite large for the small home, as was the man within the frame. He was tall, broad of frame, and dressed in a long blue coat with gold cord trim and a sash. He wore a sword at his side. His hair was long and black, falling in curls below his shoulders, and below the tricorne he wore, he looked out at the world with deep, storm-dark eyes.

"He was a great ship captain, famous in his day. Such a daring and adventurous fellow was he! Not all of his ventures were quite legal or moral, I fear. They say I have the look of him, although not the coloring, and I feel my face is more of a reflection of my dear mother's. But be it as it may, he is my forefather. His name was Adolphus Cedric Nye."

Cora, who was fixated on the forceful image of the man, was brought back from her reverie when she heard the name.

"His name seems to fit his character. Adolphus Cedric Nye sounds very much like a ship captain's name."

"I had not thought of that. I believe you are right. There is nothing left of him now, of course, but our fancy, a lesson of sorts. Although I did possess his snuffbox until lately. Quite tragically, I lost it only yesterday."

Cora looked at him in surprise. "You have lost it?"

"Yes. So now there is truly nothing left of my grandfather Nye save this portrait and my stories, I am afraid."

"But, Reverend, I believe I have found it! It has his initials on it, does it not? Adolphus . . . Cedric . . . Nye. *A, C, N.* Oh, dear! And I thought it belonged to Alexander and sent it to him only today!"

"The Lord be praised! Where did you find it, my dear?"

"On the bluff overlooking the sea . . ." She paused, gazing at Reverend Nye, and sudden caution gripped her. *Absurd*, she thought. But perhaps not. "Near Wintercroft. That seems odd. Were you walking there?"

The reverend's face was strangely expressionless.

"I do walk on occasion. It helps me to reflect upon things. The cliffs by the sea are extraordinarily inspiring, do you not think? Just looking upon the Seven Sisters—as well as Beachy Head—makes me consider the marvel of God's creation."

Cora took a cautious breath. "It does seem rather far for you to walk."

The light had been slowly failing, and as no candles had yet been lit, the reverend's form had been falling into shadow. Then, in a flash, Cora made a connection in her mind.

The reverend indeed had an impressive form— more truly appreciated in silhouette. She suddenly realized that the reverend could have been the gentleman who had left the maze with Joanna.

"What are you thinking, my dear?"

"Nothing. Nothing at all. Just . . . how odd it is how everything seems to connect. I did not grow up here, so of course it is new to me."

He sighed. "That may be remedied, and in time it shall be. But as for now, we really must marry with all haste. Would you object to doing so tonight?"

"But you have Mrs. Cooper staying with us, and you are sending to the reverend in the next parish to do the service. How could we possibly marry tonight?"

"Very simply. We shall have a ship captain wed us."

"A ship captain!"

"Come, my dear. I do know you have some thought or other that I might be connected with the local smuggling ring. It has occurred to me that it is best to own to it. You shall know the truth in time, after all. As for the ship captain, he is at anchor some way out, and if we make speedy preparations, we will be able to have our service said before many hours have passed."

"I do not know if I am in favor of this!"

"I shall explain all, I promise. I have my reasons for what I do, and they are not selfish ones."

He caught her wrist in a gentle but inescapable grip.

"Forgive me. I must be certain of your accompanying me, and so I must secure you for a very short while. Then we shall row out to the ship."

Chapter Sixteen

"*I* have gathered you all together," said Lord Wintercroft, "to inform you that Miss MacLaren is gone. Potts will confirm that my *son*"—here he shot Alexander a dark look—"was alone with her last night. I have made the best of a bad bargain and sent her packing."

"This cannot be true!"

"Heavens!"

"I cannot believe it of you, Alexander!"

Alexander, who was standing near the seated gathering in his father's study, raised his hand. "I must enter a correction. My father knows very well that Miss MacLaren left of her own free will, after refusing marriage to either one of us. I have also explained to him that nothing untoward happened between Miss MacLaren and me. I am willing to pledge with my hand on a Bible that this is the truth."

There was a moment of silence. Then Robert spoke. "Well, where did she go? She does not have the means to travel far."

"I do not know," snapped Lord Wintercroft, "nor do I wish to know!"

"She departed sometime this morning, it seems," said Alexander, "while we were unaware."

Aunt Eliza raised her chin. "That is certainly unfortunate. She was the only one among you who was not afraid of hard work!"

Roland, who was sitting backward on his chair and engaged in balancing it on its front legs, suddenly displayed interest. "Do you say that she refused the both of you and left? Astounding. Do you know, I truly respect that woman. Imagine, one of our family walking away from money! It makes one positively shiver!"

"Roland, I am ashamed of you!" snapped Aunt Eliza. "As if all we think about is money!"

Robert cleared his throat. "I must admit that her motives seem to have been sincere. It is a wonder what she has accomplished in a few short days."

"That is very true." Joanna sighed. "Yes, you all may well look at me. I could not have done it. Therefore, I cannot fault her for it." She paused. "I admit to having had some very uncharitable thoughts about Miss MacLaren. I now state, with all of you as my witness, that this was very bad of me." Joanna dropped her gaze to the rug and stared at it dispiritedly.

There was a pause. Then Mirabelle Neadow spoke up cheerily. "Dinner is served ever so promptly now! And the rooms are finally clean!"

"That is right, dear," said Robert, patting her hand.

"Bertram hardly ever sneezes now," said Aunt

Eliza. "Is that not true, Bertram? I must say that to me that is the best blessing of all."

"A remarkable woman," said Roland. "She stops Bertram from sneezing, and it seems she even raised Potts from his bed, in an extremely timely fashion, moreover. I understand he found the both of you"— here he looked at Alexander—"returning in the wee hours, looking as if you had been recovered from a shipwreck."

"An exaggeration. We had been out walking, and it was windy and damp."

Lord Wintercroft snorted his disdain. "It is not to be discussed. It is done. I shall not hear any more of it." He then stood and brandished his cane. "Now all of you get out of my study. I want some peace!"

Alex left the study, not knowing where he meant to go. The others passed him by, and all ignored him save Roland.

"Very poorly done, old man," he said, and then continued on his way.

Alex sighed. He could not fully explain to the others the circumstances in which he had been with Miss MacLaren. He had, more or less, finally managed to explain to his father, but his father was the only person in the household whom he deemed unlikely to be involved in smuggling activities.

He had considered his success in getting his father to listen to him at last a victory, but then Miss MacLaren had been discovered to be missing.

He could only be thankful for one thing: Miss MacLaren would be safe. Alex knew where she had gone. Among the household, only little Birdie knew, and she had told him, tearfully, and had completely devastated his hopes.

Alex stood there in the hall, feeling more helpless than he had ever felt in his life. He was hopelessly, completely in love with her, and she was gone.

He clenched his teeth against the pain. Once he had sworn that he would give nothing—nothing—the power to make him feel such pain again. It had happened, however, quietly and by stealth, so that he had no idea of it until it was too late.

Miss MacLaren was the steadiness, the loyalty, and the quiet strength he had never expected to find in a woman. She was the generous, caring spirit he had felt sure did not exist. She had actually cared about *him*.

And she had cared about this place and the assortment of wretched people in it. She had reached them all. And astonishingly enough, she had even begun to reach his father.

His father—of whom he had been bitterly jealous. Alex realized that now. His father, it seemed, had finally found the perfect punishment for him when he had introduced Cora MacLaren as his future bride.

But now Alex had to admit defeat. In Reverend Nye she had found all the qualities she could have wished for—a gentle and kind man who would treat her with the love and tenderness she deserved. He, Alex, could never give her that. He had grown hard and bitter like his father, and it was too late for him to change.

Alex retired to his room, first attempting to write

in his journal and then to read. Both activities proved
fruitless. At long last it was late enough to retire, and
he was preparing to do so when a knock came on his
door. He called his permission and was astonished to
see old Potts enter the room.

"A parcel, sir. It is for you."

Alex stepped forward eagerly and took the small
parcel, knowing immediately that it was from Miss
MacLaren.

"Has this only just come?"

Potts sighed. "I am afraid not, sir. I was feeling
poorly when the boy brought it. I am sorry to say
that I fell asleep."

"You may go." Alex shut the door on Potts and
immediately opened the package.

In his hand lay the Reverend Nye's snuffbox. Alex
frowned. A gift? He quickly read the note.

When he finished the note, he was no longer bewildered. He was sharper than he had been in days.

The reverend had lost his snuffbox on the cliff, and
Alex could think of only one reason that he would
have been there. Cora was not safe at all. In fact, she
was very much in danger.

Cora felt that her current situation was more desperate than any she had ever been in. She was in a
small boat in a dark sea, the unwilling passenger of
a man who determinedly rowed them closer and
closer to a fate that she now wished in every way
to escape.

"I wish that I could oblige you," he was saying,
"but in good conscience, I cannot. This is a matter of

survival for these people. I understand your scruples, but men and women must eat. I have lived here all of my life, Miss MacLaren. It is the way it must be."

Cora clutched the blanket tighter around her in the back of the boat. "You do not understand what I am saying. I *cannot* bear all of this rocking and swaying. I have no stomach for boats. I have a nervous stomach."

"My dear, I cannot tell you how sorry I am, but I have no choice. We shall be married aboard ship. We shall then sail to France for a bit. You will enjoy it. And I am sure you will come to understand why I must do this for my flock."

"Is Joanna Neadow one of your flock, Reverend Nye?"

"She is, although I do not understand why you ask."

"Because I saw you leave the maze at Wintercroft with her last night."

He was silent for several strokes of the oars. "I think I am beginning to understand. I met her for business reasons only, Miss MacLaren. She kept me informed of information at Wintercroft—comings and goings, any contact there by revenue men, and anything else of note. She is one of those who is trying to survive. She lives in a very unhappy situation, and I offered her a way to put something aside so she may escape. Do you feel she should be punished?"

Cora pressed her lips together. She was beginning to feel quite ill, but the reverend seemed not to believe her.

"She reminds me very much of another young

woman," the reverend said quietly. "She was trapped also and desperate for a way to mend her mistake. She was Alexander's mother. I could not permit Joanna to share the same fate."

As desperate as she was and as ill as she felt, this was something that Cora wished to know. "What happened to Alexander's mother?"

It was a moment before he answered. "She was a lovely young lady who was very unhappy in her marriage. I ministered to her as her vicar, and I counseled her as well as I could. A very sad story that I should not wish to see repeated."

Poor Joanna, Cora thought. As the widow of Lord Wintercroft's son, she was not bound to Wintercroft in the way that Alexander's mother had been, but she was trapped nevertheless. And she, Cora, would now be trapped because she had refused to believe Alexander when he told her he was not having an affair with Joanna.

She would very soon be Mrs. Reverend Nye.

Alex pounded on the vicar's door until he was answered by a very frightened Mrs. Cooper, in her nightgown and clutching a guttering candle. Far from reassuring her, he pushed his way into the cottage and closed the door.

"I want to see Miss MacLaren."

Mrs. Cooper fluttered her hand nervously. "You can't. She's not here."

"I *know* she is here. Do not put me off! She is staying with Reverend Nye. I must see her immediately!"

"But she isn't here! I'm tellin' you the truth! They're gone."

Alex steadied himself. *Gone.* What could have happened? Where were they at such an hour?

"Tell me where they have gone, Mrs. Cooper."

Mrs. Cooper began to cry.

"Please listen. I know what the reverend does. I understand that you are sworn to secrecy. But there is no secret." Alex leaned close to her and gently placed his hand over hers. "I am not interested in causing any trouble. I am only interested in Miss MacLaren. Please trust me. Her family needs her. *I* need her. And if I do not find her tonight, she will be unhappy for the rest of her life."

Mrs. Cooper sniffed and wiped her eyes. "They have gone to Birling Gap. They will be rowing out to board a ship and be married by the captain. That's what the reverend said."

"Is that all?"

"He said not to expect him for a fortnight. They will be sailing for France."

Alexander lost no time. He mounted Mischief and covered the mile to Birling Gap with all speed. Once there, he faced the dark cove, faintly lit by the light of a crescent moon. Not a soul stirred that he could see. Mischief blew air through his nose and shook his head in weariness, and Alex felt the cold grip of fear.

He had lost her. They were gone.

Then he saw it. Some distance out, the moonlight glinted off a small craft.

Alex sent the startled Mischief racing down to the

fisherman's wharf. Leaping off the horse, Alex searched frantically for any boat he might commandeer and stumbled across a small rowboat at the edge of the water. In a moment he was rowing rapidly out to sea.

For several minutes he applied himself mightily to the oars before he sensed that something was wrong. Why were his feet wet?

Alex looked down and swore. The ancient boat was leaking and it was leaking fast. Throwing himself into the task, he rowed furiously, but the boat soon began to lumber and sag in the water. Alex looked ahead at the small craft he pursued and realized, with utter and complete despair, that he had lost. He could not save Miss MacLaren.

The boat listed heavily to one side. In moments it would sink.

Desperate, he cupped his hands and shouted her name. "Cora!"

Nothing came in response. Dear God, nothing!

And then he heard a sharp scream—and a splash of a body striking the water.

In the next moment his boat slipped beneath the surface.

Alex swam frantically toward the distant boat, praying that it was not Cora who was in the water but terrified that it was. His entire focus was upon saving her, with no thought to how he would do so. As he swam, he became conscious of the steady, even rhythm of oars in water and realized the sound was getting closer.

The boat was coming to him.

Who was it? Perhaps it was the reverend, coming to finish him as well. *No. Not Reverend Nye. Not the only friend of his lonely youth.*

The bow of the boat closed in upon him. He looked up and saw an oar extended over the side.

"Take hold," said a soft, familiar voice.

Alex grabbed the oar and drew himself closer, as a small feminine hand reached out to him.

"Alex, is it you?" she asked.

"Cora," he breathed. "Thank God."

He climbed into the rowboat, where Cora sat alone in possession of the oars, looking for all the world as if she had been born with them in her hands.

"Are you all—"

"Are you all right—"

They both stopped, and then Cora laughed, and Alex seized her in a powerful embrace.

"Alex! You are wetting me through!"

He sat back and gazed at her precious form, veiled as it was in darkness. "I thought I had lost you."

"You very nearly did."

Alex took the oars and gazed around at the surface of the water. "Reverend Nye? Where is he?"

"I believe he is swimming for land," she said.

"What happened?"

"I am afraid he did not believe me when I told him how very ill I become on the water. And it seems he has a very strong aversion to seasickness. It affected him so that it took very little effort to topple him from the boat."

Alex smiled in the dark. "He is a very good swimmer, fortunately."

"I am glad. He does mean well. He told me what the smuggling means to the people of the parish."

"Still, it is against the law, and those involved in it become desperate and dangerous."

"I know. It is a very hard thing to puzzle out."

"Pray, Miss MacLaren, do not puzzle on it anymore."

"Miss MacLaren? I thought I had become Cora."

"I never asked your permission. It was a transgression I can only explain by the passion of the moment."

"Oh. I see."

They gained the beach in a short while. Alex pulled the boat up on the shore and then turned to Cora. "It is two miles to Wintercroft from here. I propose that you ride Mischief and I walk—slowly, I promise."

"Oh, no. I think we should go to the reverend's. It is much closer and we may borrow his cart before he returns."

Alex could not fault the plan, and so they made the moonlit walk to the reverend's.

They arrived at a deserted cottage. Cora made quick work of bundling the few possessions she had brought and returned to the parlor to find Alex waiting for her.

"The cart is ready," he said.

They turned to the door just as it opened. Reverend Nye stepped inside and closed the door behind him.

"Please do not be alarmed," he said. "There is nothing to fear. I only beg your forgiveness."

Alex stepped forward and stopped. "You wish forgiveness? What is the meaning of this?"

"You might well ask. Well, the truth is that I have come to a decision. I shall no longer be in the business of smuggling. Someone else will take my place readily enough. There are other men who are capable leaders."

The reverend looked old and tired besides being thoroughly wet. He looked at Alex, then Cora, then Alex again. Then he walked to his chair by the fireplace and sat down.

"I cannot understand this," Alex said. "A short while ago you were going to marry Cora and spirit her away to France to protect yourself."

"But I do understand," Cora said.

Both men looked at her.

"It is the portrait of your grandfather, Reverend Nye," she said. "I didn't understand why it so fascinated me before, but now I see." She looked at Alex, who gazed at her with puzzlement in his eyes.

"Alex," Cora said, "go to the top of the stairs and look at the portrait you will see there. I believe it will give you an answer."

"Yes," the reverend said. "I had forgotten that. I should have put it away years ago."

He stood and turned to face Alex. "You are the very image of my grandfather, you see." He drew a slow breath. "I shall not fight you," he said, "for a man does not raise arms against his own son."

Chapter Seventeen

C ora was alarmed by Alexander's distress. He was wordless during the entire trip home, and on arrival bid her good night and went straight to his room. Cora was relieved to go to her own bed, but she knew that Alexander suffered from more than weariness.

Bits of his conversation with the Reverend Nye danced through her head.

"Why did you never tell me?"

"I told no one. I am sorry, Alex. It seemed for the best. It would only have caused more pain."

"More pain? My father knew I was not his son and reminded me of that fact many times. I scarcely see how I could have suffered more."

"If Lord Wintercroft had known I was your father, I should have never been able to see you. To try to make amends. I thought it best to let him believe I had only attempted to counsel your mother. And so help me God, that was all I had intended to do. But I was young, weak,

and foolish. I was too proud to believe I could be tempted, then so ashamed that I feared I was past redemption."

"You were my only friend. But I see I have only been deceived again."

"I was your friend. I am still your friend. That was, and will always be, the truth."

The next day would be one of explanations once more. Cora wondered how Lord Wintercroft would react to the information that the Reverend Nye had been the leader of a ring of smugglers; then she wondered if this should be told at all. It was done now, and if anyone were to speak against the Reverend Nye, it should be Alexander. Alexander would also have to be the one to reveal his paternity.

This left her with little to say at all.

The events of the next day, however, did not happen in any way that she had expected. In the morning it was discovered that Alexander was very ill. He had taken a chill, and it had turned into a fever during the night.

Lord Wintercroft was beside himself. He stalked about cursing careless sons, he barely noticed Cora at all, and then he shut himself into his study and would not come out.

Cora faced questions from the others and evaded them as well as she could. Then she escaped them entirely by closeting herself in the sickroom.

Father, how I wish you were here. Cora stayed by Alex's bedside, placing cool cloths upon him and mixing draughts for those times when she could make him swallow. As she gazed into his fevered

face and listened to his labored breathing, she prayed
for a miracle.

A miracle of healing—not just for his body but for
his heart.

On the third day, the vicar came to visit. Cora was
surprised to hear the news, but she learned it from
Joanna, who stopped her in the hall.

"The vicar is visiting Lord Wintercroft in his
study," she whispered. "It is about Alexander, I
know. How is he, Cora? Will he recover?"

Cora swallowed. They were just outside Alexander's room, which she had left for a moment to try
to clear the haze of fear from her brain. She, Cora,
who was never afraid, had found something to be
afraid of.

"I cannot be sure. I am hopeful. He is very strong."

It was the best she could tell Joanna, and she saw
that Joanna was not satisfied.

"He must get well. He is a good man, Cora. He
has been my friend since I came to Wintercroft. He
loved me once, you know, but I chose Arthur. I made
the wrong choice."

"Do not blame yourself. We are not perfect. We
do the best we can, and then we must forgive ourselves and go on."

"I shall go on," said Joanna. "It is the only choice
I have. Perhaps someday—" Her voice caught.

"Joanna?"

"You are so good," she said softly. "I am not.
There is . . . something I must tell you. I am afraid
you will be much shocked."

"No," Cora said, "you are as good as anyone. And I shall not in the least be shocked."

Joanna gazed at her with damp remorseful eyes. "I think you shall. It was I who closed you into the little room."

Cora blinked. Indeed, she had not expected this. "Why?"

"Because I wanted to frighten you. I knew the brandy was there, and I knew you would not find the secret door from the room to the passage to the sea. I only meant to wait a little while, then pretend to find you"—Joanna paused, seemed to struggle for her composure, then continued—"but then I was afraid to seem to discover you so easily. Oh, dear, it was such a terrible act, and I am . . . so sorry . . ."

Cora reached out and touched her arm. "I forgive you. I understand. You must not—"

But she did not finish the thought. Steps were heard coming up the stairs.

"Reverend," Joanna said softly.

"Hello, dear. How are you holding up?" He took both Joanna's hands in his.

"Not well, but I shall survive." Joanna forced a small smile for the reverend. "It is Alex whom I am worried about. What did you say to Lord Wintercroft?"

"That is between Lord Wintercroft, the good Lord, and me. But perhaps someday you will know more." He gave Joanna's hands an affectionate squeeze, then turned to Cora.

"Doctor MacLaren?" he asked with a smile.

Cora smiled weakly as she felt the pang in her

heart. "Doctor MacLaren was my father. But I seem to be the only choice."

"You do very well, and I have every confidence in you." He paused. "I have spoken with Lord Wintercroft and I have his permission to visit Alex."

"Of course."

As Reverend Nye passed her, he quietly said, "I have told him the truth." Then he entered his son's room.

A day passed. Finally, on the dawning of the fifth day, Alex opened his eyes.

"Miss MacLaren?" he asked weakly.

"Yes, it is I."

He sighed deeply. "I thought I had dreamed it."

"I recall telling you once before that I am not a dream." Cora picked up a cup of water and offered it to him.

He turned his face away. "What is it?"

"Water."

"You gave me something earlier that was not water. How can I believe you?"

"I do not lie. This is water. Drink it."

He sipped it at last, and then closed his eyes once more.

"Reverend Nye came to see you."

Alexander frowned.

"He cares for you very much."

Alexander did not respond for a moment. Then he looked at her. "How has Father been?"

"Cantankerous. Quite unbearable. He has closed himself in his study and refuses to come out. The reverend did manage to see him, however."

"Reverend visited him?" A spark of interest, and of anxiety, came over his face.

"Yes. And no one mentioned any shouting, broken glass, or bloodshed."

Alexander did not smile. Instead, a haze of pain came over his eyes.

Cora sighed as he turned away from her; then she stood and walked out of the room. She went straight to Lord Wintercroft's study and walked in.

"What do you want?" he barked.

"You." Cora stopped before him. "I understand that Reverend Nye spoke to you."

Lord Wintercroft said nothing.

"I think you should know that Alex is very angry with Reverend Nye. He feels betrayed and told him so. You are the only father that Alexander has ever known. And right now, he is very ill, and you have not once gone to visit him."

Lord Wintercroft still said nothing.

Cora waited.

Then Lord Wintercroft sighed. "Reverend Nye told me the same thing," he said at last. "Why he cares is more than I can comprehend. I suppose I—"

"Just go visit him," Cora said. "Go see your son."

Lord Wintercroft remained motionless.

Cora turned and walked from the room. She climbed the stairs and entered Alex's chamber, feeling more than a little angry. She was surprised, then, when half an hour later, Lord Wintercroft appeared at the door.

"Is he . . . ?"

"Awake? Yes."

Lord Wintercroft came and stood by the bed. Then he cleared his throat.

Alex opened his eyes.

"Are you better?" Lord Wintercroft asked.

Alex gazed at him, his expression unreadable. "Apparently I am."

"Good." Lord Wintercroft cleared his throat again. "Damned foolish thing, getting wet and not changing straight into dry clothes."

"I fear I agree."

"Do you need anything?"

"No."

"Well." Lord Wintercroft paused. "Damned odd thing about the reverend. He came to see me, you know."

"I know."

There was a long pause. Cora waited, scarcely daring to breathe.

"You are the only son I have. I raised you, and I don't want any more foolishness. No caves, no getting wet, and stay away from those bedamned cliffs!"

Alex stared at him. Then he smiled a small smile. "Very well."

"Good!" Lord Wintercroft turned toward the door and then looked back. "Get married! You won't live forever!"

He closed the door firmly behind him, and when Cora looked back at Alex, he was gazing at her with a softness in his dark eyes.

"You are the most amazing woman I have ever met."

"Thank you."

"Marry me."

She felt her heart go still. "You do not wish to marry me. We had to be trapped in a cave together for you to propose!"

He gazed steadily into her eyes. "There was a way out of the cave."

She swallowed. "Oh, Alex! *My* Alex!"

For a sick man, he sat up with amazing alacrity, and Cora knew the instant before he pulled her into his arms that he was well on his way to recovery. When he let her go, he held her at arm's length and gave her a long look.

"Well?" she asked. She smiled into his warm eyes, memorizing all the love and tenderness there.

"You have not answered my question," he persisted. "I asked you to marry me. And I demand a satisfactory answer. 'When horses fly' will not at all do."

"I am sorry, dear." Cora smiled and laid her head upon his shoulder, as his arms came reassuringly around her. She closed her eyes and sighed happily. "I was much too distracted by the horses flying by your window."

Epilogue

*T*hings had changed at Wintercroft. Some said it was a miracle, some did not. After all, Lord Wintercroft was still himself and he allowed others to know it from time to time. But when Joanna married the Reverend Nye and moved to East Dean, many of the doubters changed their minds—and when this was followed by the marriage of Lord Wintercroft's son, there was happy gossip for many weeks.

It was soon accepted that the problem between father and son was finally put to rest. Lord Wintercroft, in fact, went so far as to compliment Alexander on his fine taste in women. All of this was so amazing that it was not so very difficult to imagine, after all, that horses really could fly.

Now available from
REGENCY ROMANCE

Regency Christmas Courtship
by Barbara Metzger, Edith Layton,
Andrea Pickens, Nancy Butler, Gayle Buck
An anthology of all-new Christmas novellas to warm
your heart—from your favorite Regency authors.
0-451-21681-4

A Singular Lady
by Megan Frampton
Recently impoverished orphan Titania Stanhope must
marry money if she plans to survive. The Earl of
Oakley has money, but, in an attempt to keep gold-dig-
ging girls at bay, keeps it a secret. Then he meets
Titania, whose sharp wit and keen mind are rivaled
only by her lovely face.
0-451-21683-0

Available wherever books are sold or at
penguin.com